D1542079

LUDLOW LOST

by

Kate Robinson Dunne

TWO
PIGEONS
PRESS

TWO PIGEONS PRESS

Copies of this book can be purchased for educational purposes. For information, please write Marketing & Sales, Two Pigeons Press, 103 Michigan Avenue, Montreal, Quebec, Canada H9R 3V7

Chapter illustrations copyright © Kate Robinson Dunne, 2017.
Cover design and illustration by Julie Prescesky, based on an original concept by Kate Robinson Dunne.
Formatting and interior design by Noah Adam Paperman.

The K & Fairy Design is a trademark of Kate Robinson Dunne and is used with permission.

ISBN 978-0-9918161-6-3

for Gerrard

&

to Nana

Fairy •n. (pl. **fairies**) a small ~~imaginary~~ being of human form that has magical powers.

-ORIGIN Old French *fae*

CHAPTER 1

On Ludlow Osgoode's eleventh birthday, he was kidnapped by a fairy. Not a hundred fairies, not even a pair of fairies, but one single fairy, all on her own. You're probably wondering how a thing as small and feeble as a fairy could kidnap something as large and awkward as an eleven-year-old boy, and the answer is: with trickery, of course.

Ludlow was also quite small for his age, but that's beside the point.

The actual trick, though quite extraordinary from a human's point of view, was quite elementary from the fairy's.

Ludlow wouldn't remember the trick for some time, though. When he first came to, he was more preoccupied with figuring out where he was than how he'd gotten there.

It was so dark when he opened his eyes that he wasn't even sure they really *were* open, but slowly the interior of a wooden packing crate came into view above him; he was lying flat on his back at the bottom of it. Only a very dim light seeped in through the knotholes and cracks between the wooden slats, until he sat up, and a warm glow filled the crate as a small voice shouted, "Get off of me!"

She crawled out from under him and flew clumsily about the place, shaking out her wings and straightening her clothes.

"A fairy," he whispered.

She flitted and fled, seemingly in a panic now, from one crack of light to another, like a wasp trapped in a car.

"It can't be," Ludlow said, trying to focus his tired eyes on her as she darted past, glowing ever brighter.

"Oh, it can be," she said. "It can be, and it is."

"Is what?" he asked.

"A kidnapping," she said.

"We're being kidnapped?" he asked, only then noticing that the crate was moving.

"No! Not we. You. *You're* being kidnapped," she said. "I'm kidnapping you."

"You?" he asked, pointing. "*You're* kidnapping me?"

"Yes," she answered. "Why do you sound so unconvinced?"

"Well, if you're kidnapping me, shouldn't you be on the outside of this crate?"

"You silly boy," she said, laughing, though her hands slowly curled into fists. "Things are not always as they seem."

"Oh," he said, and was actually quite prepared to believe her until...

"Let me out!" she shrieked, slamming her raised fists into the lid of the crate. "Let me out, backstabbing two-timers!"

"Backstabbing two-timers?" Ludlow asked.

"Yes." She turned to face him again, suddenly composed. "Those are my evil henchmen."

"Henchmen?" Ludlow asked.

"Yes, my henchmen. Backstabbing and Two-timers. Goblins have funny names like that."

"Goblins?"

Goblins are quite complicated creatures for a number of reasons. If you've never had the bad, though sometimes good, fortune to meet one, there are two fundamental personality traits common to all goblins that you should know before you read any further: (1) they struggle with severe bouts of forgetfulness; and (2) they are known to hold a grudge, even though they don't usually remember why.

It is also worth noting that although most goblins' names are somewhat out of the ordinary, these goblins' names were not Backstabbing and Two-timers. As Ludlow would find out, their names were actually Raghnall and Berneas.

"You know what you did," Ludlow suddenly heard one of them say.

"What do you mean?" the other answered.

"Someone's been yelling at us, Raghnall," the first one replied, "and I'm sure it's your fault."

The fairy hovered in the air, seeming to listen for the directions the voices were coming from, and finally flew up to a knothole in the side and looked out.

Ludlow felt the crate drop slightly and rise into the air again as Raghnall huffed and wheezed out the words, "Why is this crate so heavy, do you think?"

"Well, it's got a human child in it for one thing," Ludlow barely heard over the *slurps* and *pops* of their footsteps in the wet ground.

"Does it really?" Raghnall asked, almost shouting.

"It was you who tossed him in there, you ignoramus!"

"That sounds very unlike me," he said. "Why would I have done such a thing?"

"I don't remember," Berneas replied.

"It was me!" the fairy shouted through the knothole. "I forced you to do my evil bidding!"

"Someone's yelling at us," Raghnall said.

"I masterminded this whole operation," she said, turning to Ludlow. "It was all me. They're just transporting you." The crate jerked once more. "And they're not even doing a good job of *that*."

Indeed, Ludlow was finding the trip quite bumpy and unpleasant, as you can imagine travelling in a packing crate might be—especially when your only company is a disgruntled fairy, and you have no idea where you're going or whether you will ever return.

Apart from being tossed about inside the crate, which felt quite real, the whole ordeal was like something out of a dream. The thought occurred to Ludlow that he may have suffered a blow to the head, knocking him unconscious, or that he was asleep and dreaming and these creatures didn't exist except in his own imagination. This is the typical human response when confronted with creatures human beings don't believe in and, in fact, Ludlow *was* quite groggy, as if he'd just awoken from a deep sleep.

He tried closing his eyes tight and opening them again a number of times, but every time he opened them the fairy was still there, hovering above him with her arms crossed, and "Backstabbing" and "Two-timers" could still be heard grumbling outside.

"Where are they taking us?" Ludlow finally asked.

"To the ship," the fairy answered.

"Oh," he said, and then realized he still had no idea. "What ship?"

"You certainly ask a lot of questions," she said, landing on his bent knee. "If you must know," she pointed towards another knothole, "it's a goblin ship called the *Anathema*." Though Ludlow strained his neck he couldn't yet see the ship. He opened his mouth to ask another question but the fairy cut him off. "And, before you ask," she said, "I don't know where it's going. We have a deal. This time, I'm leaving the crew before they shove off."

"Are you sure?" Ludlow asked, leaning back.

"Of course I'm sure! Why wouldn't I be sure?"

"They've trapped you inside a packing crate."

"Let me out!" she squealed, leaping from his knee. Her head disappeared through a knothole in the lid, but with a thud it reappeared, and with a groan she came hurtling back down towards him and landed unconscious in his lap.

"Fairy," he said, as he picked her up by the hood of her tunic. He pressed her tiny body against his ear to listen for a breath. It was faint, but a fairy's breathing always is. Then he heard her heartbeat. He tried gently shaking her awake, but it didn't do any good; she was as limp as a rag doll. He cradled her in his hands and watched her glow flicker like a loose light bulb. Now that she was still, he was finally able to get a close look at her. She was fair skinned with raven black hair, wearing a green hooded tunic and trousers, and tiny black slippers on her feet. He carefully turned her over to reveal her wings. They were nothing like the insect wings he had seen on fairies in picture books; they were long and gold-feathered, almost like the wings of his canary, Joey.

Without thinking, he slowly closed his fingers around her as he did when removing Joey from his cage. He thought he'd probably never see Joey again or his dog, Toby, or his parents. Then he realized he might never see his grandmother again. In the whole eleven years of his life he had never felt loneliness the way he did at that moment.

Though the fairy was unpleasant company, he actually found himself wishing she would wake up just as he felt her squirming between his fingers and heard her muffled voice trying to shout, "As your kidnapper, I order you to release me!"

He spread his fingers and she flew right back to the same knothole. "Are we almost there?" she yelled.

"What did she say?" Raghnall asked.

"Who?" Berneas asked.

"I can't take much more of this," the fairy said, burying her face in her hands.

CHAPTER 2

There are two things you should know about Ludlow Osgoode before you read any further: (1) he started reading earlier than most children and was quite clever as a result (By his eleventh birthday he had read fairy tales, mystery novels and volumes A through T of his grandfather's *Encyclopaedia Britannica*.); and (2) although he was small for his age, he was resourceful and stronger than he looked.

While the fairy wasn't looking, Ludlow stretched his arms out and pressed lightly against the sides of the crate. No movement. He pressed harder. Nothing. He felt along the corners for a gap wide enough to get his fingers into, hoping to pry it open somehow, but there wasn't a single one. It was sealed tight. He noticed a knothole in the base of the crate between his legs, and felt the pockets of his cardigan and trousers for something, *anything* he could drop through the hole to leave a trail, but they were empty except for a bit of crumpled tissue. Then he heard what sounded like voices outside that weren't Backstabbing's or Two-timers. Distant voices, some of which had to be human, he was almost certain.

The crate tilted and Ludlow slid into its side, his face pressed against a knothole. When he opened his eyes, through the left one he finally saw their destination.

The *Anathema* was a centuries-old tall ship docked at Princess Pier. Ludlow had read about tall ships in the encyclopaedia, but had never been so close to one. Under different circumstances, he might have thought it quite beautiful. Despite the spitting rain and late hour, it had attracted the eye of a number of passers-by who stopped to admire the craftsmanship of times gone by. Curiously, they were unfazed by the fact that it was crawling with goblins. Some even stopped the goblin crew to ask questions about the ship. One would have expected the onlookers to ask questions such as "What's happened to your face?" or, "Have you been in a terrible, disfiguring accident?" or, "Have you considered shaving that?" or even, "Are you a goblin?" instead of the more popular, "What's this ship's top speed?" or, "Are those the original sails?" or even, "Are the cannons still functional?"

It was a glorious tall ship by all accounts, but still one would expect folk to be slightly taken aback by the sight of the crew. The reason they weren't is partly the reason Ludlow found himself trapped in a packing crate. To humans, the goblins didn't look like goblins at all. Even Ludlow couldn't make out a single goblin amongst the crowd. They all looked like people: ordinary, everyday, unremarkable people—thanks to a fairy named Adhair, who had enchanted the entire crew.

In case you've never had the bad, though sometimes good, fortune to meet a fairy, you should know that all fairies possess some sort of magic, each one different from the other. In Adhair's case, she was able to alter human beings' perceptions of creatures, places and time. It was a gift that she had never found particularly useful herself but one that made other creatures who ordinarily hid from humans wish to possess her.

Ludlow could make out faces and bits of conversations as they drew closer to the crowded pier. He opened his mouth to shout, then hesitated. He looked back at Adhair, whose face was still buried in her open palms. He looked out again. He took a deep breath. "Help!" he tried to shout out, but didn't hear a sound. "Help me!" he tried again. Still not a word seemed to come out of his mouth, though he felt his lips moving and the breath surge out of him. "I'm being kidnapped! I'm in the packing crate!" He punched and kicked silently against the sides as he tried yet again. "Heeeeeeelllllp!"

"They can't hear you, you know," Adhair huffed. He looked back at her through teary eyes to see that her hands were now firmly clamped over her ears. "I can, though," she said, as she removed them. "So cut it out."

"I think the crate is shouting at us, Berneas," they heard Raghnall say.

CHAPTER 3

After another bumpy stretch of the journey, it was Ludlow's turn for a knock to the head when the crate was finally dropped onto the deck of the *Anathema*. Everything, including Adhair, seemed to be spinning when he opened his eyes, but she was actually still firmly camped at the knothole, looking out as she had been for some time.

"Bernie, I demand to be let out of here this instant. I want what was promised to me," she said.

A large, hazel-coloured eye appeared at the knothole, and a horrible smell wafted in and filled the crate. The smell of goblins can only be described as a cross between the smell of dirty socks and wet socks that have been allowed to go mouldy, which is curious, because goblins don't even wear socks.

"Oh, hello, Harry," Raghnall said to her. "What are you doing in there?"

"You tossed me in here with him. That wasn't the plan. I wish I could enchant you to have more than a five-second memory!" she shouted.

"That doesn't sound right," Berneas said.

"What doesn't?" she asked.

"That was the plan. It was the plan, indeed. I even wrote it down," Berneas said. There was a rustling of papers and then, "Yes, that's right. Step one: Adhair—that's you— kidnaps human child," she read. "Step two: Raghnall and Berneas—that's us—intercept Adhair and human child."

"What's that supposed to mean?" Adhair asked. "You were supposed to assist me, not intercept me."

"Intercept. Good word, that is," Raghnall said.

"Step three: Raghnall and Berneas capture Adhair and human child in packing crate and return to ship."

"Whose plan is that?" Adhair asked.

"Morag's," Berneas answered.

"That backstabbing two-timer," she said, shaking her head. "Is there a fourth step to her plan?"

"Can you read that?" Berneas asked.

"Didn't you write it?" Raghnall asked.

"I can't remember," Berneas said. "Just read it."

"Step four: Dump Adhair...and human child into...the sforaje rum? Storage rom? Storage room," Raghnall read. "That's it. Storage room."

"Raghnall," the fairy said.

"Yes, Harry?"

"You used to be my favourite," she said.

"Thank you, Harry," he said. Ludlow felt the crate being slowly shoved along the deck of the ship as Raghnall asked, "Isn't she sweet?"

"I don't think she is actually, but I can't remember why," Berneas answered, just as the crate tipped over the edge of a staircase and, after quite a few more knocks to

Ludlow's head, elbows, knees and various other body parts, smashed to pieces at the bottom.

He pushed away the broken planks of wood and looked around, trying to catch a glimpse of the goblins, but the hatch had already dropped closed above them. In the dark he could only make out parts of the room as Adhair darted past illuminating the shadowy corners as she flew from one to another. It was, indeed, a storage room; Adhair's glow revealed other intact crates, barrels strung together with rope, shelves stacked high with loaves of bread, and empty burlap sacks piled on the floor before she finally came to rest on a stair and cried into her sleeve.

Ludlow thought maybe he should try to console her, but by now he was fairly sure that if he did, she would just remind him she was his kidnapper and therefore didn't need consoling.

Over Adhair's whimpering, he heard hordes of goblins muttering above deck, the sound of wet ropes slapping down into puddles, and then the clink and rattle of metal chain links and a loud, lingering, dripping splash: the anchor being raised. He grabbed Adhair by the legs and used her to light his way around the room. He climbed to the top of the stairs and tried to push the hatch open, first with his fist and finally by pressing against it with his back.

"There's no way out!" Adhair yelled. "Unhand me this instant."

"There has to be a way out!" Ludlow yelled back at her. "You got me into this, now you get me out of it."

"You got yourself into this," she replied, "and as much as I'd like to get out of here, there is no way out."

Ludlow held her up to his face and saw that she was still crying. She reached back and pulled her hood down over her eyes, but he had already seen her tears, small though they were. He set her down on the stair beside him and listened as the gangway was pulled back onto the ship, and onlookers from the shore shouted their wishes to the crew for a safe journey, from which Ludlow wasn't sure he would ever return.

"There are people out there watching. How did the goblins get past all those people unnoticed?" he asked. "Or do goblins not look the way I think they look?"

"I don't know how you think they look," she said with a sniffle. "I suppose they look like human beings. Short, greyish, hairy human beings with pointy ears and snouts."

"Snouts," he repeated.

"I suppose they don't look that much like human beings," she said.

"Do they wear clothes?" he asked.

"Of course they wear clothes. They're not animals."

"But they look like clothed animals?" he asked.

"Well, yes, but not to those human beings out there. To them the goblins look just like other human beings. Ugly ones, mind you, but human beings just the same. I've enchanted them. It'll wear off soon," she sighed, "but not before we're well away from here."

"You've cast a spell? On the humans?"

"In a way," she answered.

"Like you did in the crate?" he asked. "When I couldn't hear myself?"

"Exactly."

"Can you make them smell better?" he asked.

"Only to you. If I could make them smell better to me, I would've done it already," she said.

There was an awkward silence between them until they felt the jolt of the ship launching, and Ludlow finally dared to ask, "Who's Morag?"

"Morag's the captain of this ship," Adhair said, rising into the air and circling the room once more. "She's a banshee."

"Banshees are real?" he asked. She stopped mid-air and looked at him, most likely waiting for him to remember that he was talking to a fairy and had been transported to a ship by goblins, which he eventually did. "Sorry," he said.

For those of you who have never had the bad fortune to meet or hear a banshee, you should know that a banshee is a spirit whose wailing cries foretell, or even cause, an imminent death. It's a horribly depressing thing to be, and as a result banshees are often depressed and spiteful creatures who are generally unwelcome, especially at parties, which makes them even more depressed and spiteful.

"Well, what does a banshee want with me?" Ludlow asked.

"She loves children," Adhair replied. She paced in a circle atop a pile of burlap sacks, digging her heels into it and fluffing the topmost sack into a kind of pillow. "Night," she said with a yawn and laid down and closed her eyes.

"You're just going to go to sleep?" Ludlow asked.

"What do you suggest I do?" she asked, opening her eyes again. "They won't let us out until we're a good hour's flight from any shore. That's how they keep me here."

"I don't understand."

She sighed deeply. "I can only fly a certain distance before I get tired and have to land," she said. "Once we're far enough out to sea, they'll let us out of here, because I won't be able to fly away, and you won't be able to swim away."

"Oh," he said.

"I'm going to sleep now," she said, pulling the hood of her tunic over her head.

"I'm Ludlow, by the way."

"Adhair," she replied.

"What does that mean?"

"Well, if you looked it up in a dictionary the definition would probably be: 'the name of a fairy who's angry about being lied to by banshees and goblins and tired of answering little boys' questions and just wants to go to sleep'."

"Oh, Adhair's your name," he realized.

"I prefer to be called Harry." She yawned and closed her eyes once more.

"Harry?" he asked. "What did you mean when you said 'you got yourself into this'?"

"Don't you remember?"

"No."

"You will."

CHAPTER 4

Ordinarily, Ludlow had no trouble falling asleep. He usually drifted to sleep after a few sips of weak tea with milk, and after nestling under a heap of soft blankets to the sound of his grandmother's voice telling stories of heroes and heroines and creatures human beings don't believe in. You can understand that it would be fairly easy to fall asleep under those conditions. Presently, however, Ludlow found himself on a cold hard floor, wrapped in scratchy hole-ridden burlap sacks, trying hard not to imagine the banshee he'd meet the next morning (whether she loved children or not), and trying even harder not to breathe through his nose.

He lay awake for what seemed like hours, listening to muffled conversations, the creaking of the ship and the sounds of the sea. What little light had filtered into the room from lamps and lanterns outside was slowly snuffed out until the only light to be seen was the dim glow of Harry, asleep on a mound of empty sacks at arm's length from him, and shivering beneath her puffed out wings.

She must be used to this, Ludlow thought, watching her. She let out a small cough and tucked her face under a wing. *She doesn't need my help*, he thought, *she's my kidnapper*. As he turned away from her, he thought he heard a sound. He held his breath, trying to hear it again. It was the faint chattering of a fairy's tiny teeth.

She kidnapped me. He pulled the burlap over his head. *Serves her right*. He pushed the sacks away from his face again. *She doesn't deserve my help*, he thought, and reached up, plucked her from atop the pile of sacks and set her down on his chest.

CHAPTER 5

L udlow awoke to find himself seated on the antique chair in the front hallway of his house. Toby trotted slowly past him to the front door and looked out through the frosted pane of glass. He always did that. The brown and white spaniel sat and titled his head sideways to scratch his floppy ear with his hind leg, then stood up and walked back towards Ludlow and stopped in a pile of rain boots. Sitting on boots and shoes was another thing Toby always did. Why he did that, Ludlow hardly knew, but all creatures are different, aren't they? Dogs probably wonder any number of things about humans, including why they wear clothes, why they wash themselves so often and why they aren't sent into a blind panic at the smell of the postman.

There certainly were a lot of rain boots in the front hall. Ludlow wondered why. Then he noticed the umbrella stand was so full of umbrellas that some had just been left open to rest on the tile floor. How could his mother allow open umbrellas in the house? It's very bad luck, or so she always said but never explained why. Actually, it's not so much to do with luck as it is common sense. You could break a light fixture or poke someone's eye out. Nevertheless, something quite out of the ordinary must have been going on for Ludlow's mother to allow open umbrellas in the house.

Where is my mother, anyway? he wondered. *Where's Nana? Why am I sitting alone in the front hallway?*

He looked down the hall towards the spare room door and then into the kitchen at the back of the house. He saw shadows moving and heard hushed voices, but couldn't make out whose shadows they were or what was being said. An umbrella snapped shut. It startled him. Toby lay down in the pile of boots and made a strange grumbling sound he had never made before. Another umbrella snapped shut. The front door swung open wide and the bright light of day shut his eyes tight once more.

CHAPTER 6

*L*udlow awoke to find himself still nestled under layers of empty burlap sacks with Harry curled up in a ball, asleep on his chest. The hatch was open, filling the room with sunlight and the salty taste of sea air. The whole night had passed, a whole night of distance between home and wherever they were now.

"Adhair," he whispered. She didn't move. "Harry," he said the second time, nudging her chin with his finger. She was suddenly wide awake and within seconds had made her escape through the hatch. The sounds of a great row arose on the deck above, and Ludlow waited down below, listening.

"Backstabbing" was the first word he could make out and then "plan," "freedom" and "stupid goblins."

Just then, one of the stupid goblins peered down at him from the open hatch and extended a hairy paw-like hand towards Ludlow.

"Might as well come up, human. It's nicer up here, even with all the yelling." He smiled, or at least, Ludlow thought he was smiling. He looked just as Harry had described and smelled just the way Ludlow remembered. He'd have been terrifying if only he wasn't so friendly. Ludlow got to his feet and climbed the stairs and let the hairy creature help him up onto the deck.

The main deck was almost abandoned except for the two of them and one little goblin swabbing the deck with the dirtiest mop Ludlow had ever seen. He stopped mopping and gave a little wave. The argument between Harry and the goblins had moved back to the quarterdeck but could still be heard throughout the ship.

"Lovely day, isn't it?" the first goblin said, closing the hatch behind Ludlow.

"You're the goblin who tossed me in the crate, aren't you?" Ludlow asked.

"I don't remember that, but it doesn't make it untrue," he answered. He pulled a pair of fogged up eyeglasses from his face and wiped them with the sleeve of his tattered shirt. When he put them back on, they were almost dirtier than before he'd polished them.

"You are. I recognize your voice," Ludlow said.

"Oh, yes," he said, seeming to recognize him now that he'd cleaned his glasses. "I'm Raghnall."

"Right. I'm Ludlow," he replied.

"Pleased to meet you. I'm Raghnall," Raghnall replied.

"I know, you just said that."

"Did I? I'm sorry," he said, shaking his head. "We goblins forget things sometimes, but we always remember them eventually."

"How would you know? You could forget something completely and never know you'd known it *or* forgotten it."

"You're quite clever for a human," Raghnall said.

"Thank you, I think," Ludlow replied.

"Oh no, she won't like that," Raghnall explained. "If I were you, I'd pretend to be a bit simple-minded. It'll make life easier for all of us. Not too simple-minded, though. She has no patience for idiots. Come with me."

Ludlow followed Raghnall along the upper deck, looking from side to side as he went. He couldn't see a speck of land or a single boat on the horizon, and there wasn't a bird or even a cloud in the sky. Above them towered great masts supporting vast, billowing sails, and another little goblin who sat perched on the main topmast looking through a nautical telescope, no doubt at some more empty water and sky.

Raghnall led Ludlow to another staircase, then across the quarterdeck and up to the poop deck. On a post at the top of the stairs hung a rusty birdcage with a cross-armed and scowling Harry perched on a swing inside it. Beyond her, from amongst a horde of grumbling goblins, rose what resembled a human woman but was actually a banshee.

She walked towards him through the mass of goblins, seeming to walk right through some and pushing others out of her way. Her hair sprouted out of her head and grew around her to her feet like a winding, woody vine. It was coarse and knotted with the knots of a tree, not those of human hair, and the ends were split and spread like roots around the hem of her gown. In the light, she was turquoise as glass, but murky as pond water. Still, you could see right through her if the light was just so. When she drifted into the shadows of the sails, though, she glowed emerald and appeared as real and alive as Ludlow himself.

She circled him, looking him up and down, and then stopped in front of Harry to ask, "Is he defective? His mouth does not appear to close."

Ludlow closed his mouth.

"Oh, good," she said. "Are you sure he is a human boy? He looks somewhat elf-like." She pulled his hair away from his ears, his un-pointy, human ears. She leaned in and sniffed his head and instantly recoiled. "Ugh," she gasped. "He certainly stinks of a human boy."

"*I* stink?" Ludlow asked.

"You will speak when you are spoken to, boy!" she shouted. An icy draft swirled momentarily around her, and her eyes seemed to flash violet before fading back to green. "But yes," she said when she'd regained her composure. "You stink of a human boy, and they stink of goblins," she said, shuddering. "It is a subtle difference but a difference nevertheless." She pulled and tugged at his cardigan and the collar of his shirt as she asked, "What is your name, human?"

Ludlow was speechless. Of course he knew his own name, but somehow he couldn't make a sound.

Morag stared at him.

"What are you waiting for?" Harry asked in a loud whisper. "Tell her your name."

Morag still stared.

He looked to Harry, then Raghnall and then to the rest of the crew, who all stared back at him, anxious looks on their faces, but still he couldn't bring himself to say a word.

"I think...his name is Ludlow," Raghnall finally said.

"Was I speaking to you?" Morag spun around to face Raghnall as a gust of icy wind rushed past her.

"No. My apologies, your malevolence," he answered with an awkward bow.

"Do you not have something else you should be doing, Rag?"

"It's Raghnall, ma'am," he said.

"Fine," she said, as a wave crashed against the side of

the ship. "Raghnall."

He stared at her blankly.

"Well?"

"Sorry. What was the question?" he asked.

"Awaaaaaaaay!" she wailed.

No two banshees' wails sound exactly the same, although each produces similarly violent results. Morag's wail sounded like that of a screaming baby in an ambulance, sirens blaring and tires screeching against slick roads through a wild, driving storm.

"Not again," Raghnall said, stumbling backwards down the stairs.

Waves rose up from the sea and hugged the sides of the ship, lifting it into the air. The goblin crew rushed and tumbled across the decks, some lowering the sails, others clamouring to ready the lifeboats. Ludlow fell back against the railing and grabbed onto Harry's cage to steady himself as the boat lurched and then dropped back down into the sea. All was suddenly quiet. He looked around to see most of the goblin crew staring at him again. What they were waiting for this time, Ludlow hardly knew. He didn't have much time to wonder about it, though. Suddenly, he was too occupied with vomiting over the side of the ship to care about anything else.

"You all know what happens when you make me angry," he heard Morag say. "Adhair, why can you not enchant these creatures to have more than a five-second memory?" she asked, as the sound of her voice and footsteps faded down the stairs.

"She's gone," Harry said softly.

"Am I...dying?" Ludlow asked.

"I doubt it," Harry answered. "You're too young and healthy for it to kill you. How much do you actually know about banshees?" she asked, but he only grunted in response.

"Right, well," she said "when they wail, humans die. Sometimes they wail because they sense a human nearby is about to die, and other times they wail and it causes someone's death. And she wails a lot."

Ludlow grunted again.

"I have nothing against most humans, neither do the goblins," she explained. "I think I speak for all of us when I say we definitely don't want anyone to die. So we try to just keep her happy at all times, never upset her, but it's so hard when half the crew forgets what they've been ordered to do from one moment to the next and carry on arguments for years without even remembering why they're arguing. It's insanity aboard this ship, so that doesn't work."

Ludlow nodded.

"So you've noticed?" she said. "We're lucky if they even remember their own names half the time."

Ludlow let out a moan that almost sounded like the question he was trying to ask.

"Why don't we avoid humans then?" she'd understood. "Well," she said, "we can't avoid human contact altogether. At sea we pass other ships, ferries and fishing boats. We keep our distance, but still we need to go ashore for supplies, like fresh water, flour and medicine, and to kidnap children, of course. Anyway, as I said, you're young and healthy like that other one was, so it should only make you a bit sick to your stomach."

Although Ludlow wasn't in a position to correct her at that moment, the expression "a bit sick to your stomach" was a glaring understatement. If you've ever had stomach flu or been sea sick, you'll almost understand how Ludlow was feeling. If you've ever had both at once, you'll understand exactly how he was feeling. His stomach was twisting in knots, his legs were shaking and his head was spinning. He barely opened his eyes for fear he would vomit again and was almost asleep with his head on the railing for some time. Only when he was fairly certain he wouldn't throw up again, did he finally speak words.

"What happened...to the other one?"

"Other what?" she asked.

"You said 'young and healthy like the other one.' Was there another kid, before me?"

"Yes. He escaped, though."

"How?" he asked.

"Nobody knows. One night he was here, the next morning he wasn't," she answered. "All four lifeboats were accounted for. It's a mystery. What was his name?" she asked herself. "Maddy or something. Does that sound like a human name?" Ludlow finally opened his eyes to see her standing on the railing, offering him a dirty rag. "It's actually the cleanest one," she said with a shrug.

Ludlow wiped his mouth and chin with the cloth and slid down the wall until he was seated on the deck of the ship. The goblins had scattered and seemed to be going about their business, hoisting the sails, polishing the rails with more dirty rags and mopping the decks as if nothing had happened—they probably didn't remember what had happened anyway.

"I should have known they wouldn't let me go," Harry said, fluttering back up to her birdcage. "They can't even drop anchor near a human settlement without me enchanting them."

"Where would you have gone?" Ludlow asked.

"Home," she answered, "to Kensington Gardens." She was now perched on her swing once more.

"Do you have any idea how he did it?" Ludlow asked.

"How who did what?" she asked. "The one that got away?"

"Exactly."

"No," she answered. "I wish I did."

"Human!" Morag shouted from the foot of the stairs. "Come to my cabin."

Ludlow looked to Harry.

"That's you," Harry said, nodding towards the stairs with a frown.

He reached up. He clasped a hand around the railing.

He dragged himself to his feet, one at a time, moving as slowly as he possibly could.

"Now!" Morag shouted.

He bolted down the stairs quick as lightning.

CHAPTER 7

As you may recall, Ludlow was quite clever (and resourceful) for a human, and as he looked around Morag's cabin, he was already considering an escape plan of his own. Being the quarters of a banshee rather than those of a human ship's captain, it was quite unlike any captain's cabin you may imagine. Its totally uncomfortable looking unslept-in bunk was draped in cobwebs and rested under a thick layer of dust, as did almost everything else in the room except a path she had worn in the floor, no doubt from pacing through sleepless nights. Banshees, being undead spirits, don't sleep.

She drifted over to a small wooden cart that overflowed with bottles of ointments and pills; some were old glass bottles, stopped with corks and filled with fog, that looked like they'd been salvaged from a shipwreck. Others looked so new they might have been stolen from a hospital just the day before. Of all the strange things about these quarters, this was, indeed, the strangest.

"I do not know what any of this is for," she said, plucking bottles from the top tray and squinting to read the labels.

Ludlow noticed a number of objects on a table in the center of the room, a compass among them. *A compass could help me find the way home*, he thought. His father had taught him how to use one.

"What does that say?" Morag asked, shoving a bottle into his face. "It looks like it says Proplaxinolthinophalynite. What is that?"

"I don't know," he answered, trying to read the ridiculously long word himself. "But the skull and crossbones symbol probably isn't a good sign."

"Pirates?" she asked.

"Or poison," he answered.

"Hmm. That does seem more likely," she said, putting it back and drawing up another. "This one has some fungus in it," she said, holding it up to the light of the window.

Banshees, in case you hadn't noticed, are terrible at nursing people back to health, and are definitely not qualified to prescribe medication.

"I actually feel much better now," Ludlow said, though it was a gross exaggeration. "I could use some rest in a proper bed, though," he said, and dropped into a painful wooden chair by the table.

"So, you are quite ill then?" she asked. "I am sorry about that, but you will have to get used to it. It will happen whenever I start keening."

"Keening, ma'am?" he asked.

"Yes, keening, wailing, lamenting," she said. She reached a hand out to feel his forehead, but he instantly flinched away from her.

"Your hand's ice cold," he said.

"Is it?" she asked, putting it up to her own forehead. "Of course it is. I am an undead spirit," she said. "You are sure you do not need any of this medicine?" she asked, pushing the cart towards him.

"No, thank you," he shook his head. "I just need to lie down," Ludlow said.

"In a moment," she said, beginning to pace, following the path in the dust. "First, I must make one thing clear. There will be no escaping this ship."

"I wouldn't dream of it, ma'am," he answered.

"Would you not?" she asked. "You might feel differently after you have been here awhile. Your stay here will be unpleasant, to say the least." She stopped and stood across the table from him. "I love children," she said with an awkward smile.

"You do?" he asked.

"Indeed. I have always longed for a child of my own. A little boy or girl to dress in suffocating clothes..."

"Suffocating?"

"I meant comfortable, yet stylish," she said. "I would feed them live scorpion rolls and poisoned soup..."

"Human children couldn't eat those things," Ludlow interrupted her again. "They'd die."

"Of course," she said, though she seemed flustered. "I meant sausage rolls and green pea soup...with a hint of mint, and lemon tartlets for dessert," she said. "I would play games with them like run for your life..."

"Do you mean tag?" he asked.

"...and hide and sleep forever," she said.

"Seek," Ludlow said. "Hide and seek."

"Exactly," she said, and then cleared her throat. "As

I said, I am sorry that my keening will make you ill from time to time," she said with another smile so crooked it was almost sideways, "but you will recover. Apart from the fever and vomiting, which will be excessive and most unpleasant, if you behave and do not try to escape, no other harm will come to you."

Ludlow was relieved for a moment, until she placed both hands on the table and leaned across it to whisper between cold breaths, "But mark my words, if you escape, I will hunt you down and I will end you. Understood?"

"Yes, ma'am," he said, trembling.

"Now for your lie down. I will put you in the quarters of Raghnall for the time being," she said, backing into a shadow and glowing a vibrant green. "Raghnall will sleep in hammock twenty-three tonight, as he should," she said, pacing again. "When you are well enough, you will have hammock twenty-four. Twenty-four will be your hammock and no other. Understood?"

Ludlow nodded.

"Good little beast," she said, and disappeared out onto the deck.

Ludlow moved quickly around the table, collecting

everything he might need that could fit into the pockets of his cardigan: the compass, a pocket telescope and a small metal tube he hoped was filled with matches. By the time Raghnall appeared in the doorway, Ludlow was nestled in the crook of the painful chair once more.

"You've only been awake half an hour and you're already going back to bed?" Raghnall scooped him up in his arms. "I think he's ill, ma'am," he said, as they passed Morag on the quarterdeck.

"I just told you that," she said. "Remain calm," she said to herself, closing her eyes. "Remain calm."

CHAPTER 8

Raghnall's "quarters" were not what Ludlow had expected, although Ludlow wasn't quite sure what he had expected. What should a goblin's quarters look like? Would you know? In fact, the décor was quite luxurious for a room the size of a closet on the lower deck of a ship. The bed filled the entire floor, and from the edges of the bed to the ceiling the walls were covered with paintings that had, no doubt, been stolen. All were of people, none of whom Ludlow recognized. Under a porthole was a single shelf, which held an oil lamp, a twin-bell alarm clock and some old books, the pages nearly spilling out of the bindings.

Ludlow took off his cardigan, hung it on a nail and climbed into the bed. It was almost as comfortable as Ludlow's own bed at home. The blankets, though quite worn, were surprisingly soft and dry and he sank into them willingly.

"Raghnall," Ludlow began, as Raghnall reached over him to open the porthole, "can I ask you something?"

"Didn't you just ask me something?" Raghnall asked.

"What?"

"That was a question: 'Can I ask you something?'" he answered.

"Yes, I suppose it was," Ludlow said.

"Glad we got that sorted. Sleep tight then," Raghnall said, pulling the door closed.

"Wait!" Ludlow stopped him. "I have another question."

"What was the first question?" Raghnall asked.

Ludlow thought long and hard about the answer, and not just about the answer, but about the entire plan he was devising. Goblins, although not as mean and scary as he'd expected them to be, were quite exasperating, and he wasn't sure he could carry on a conversation for more than a few minutes with a goblin, let alone count on one to help him escape without giving him away.

"Sleep tight then," Raghnall said again, and again tried to shut the door.

"Raghnall, are you happy here?" Ludlow asked.

"No one's happy here, human," he answered.

"Do you know what happy is?"

"Yes. These paintings make me happy. Oh, and books. Books make me ever so happy," Raghnall said. Just then, a sheepish look came across his beastly face. He took a quick glance around, "And orange cream-filled dark chocolates," he said. "I stole some from a shop...somewhere. You can have one if you like. I keep them under the pillow. Sleep tight then," he said, and finally shut the door.

Ludlow reached up into the pocket of his cardigan and pulled out the compass. Its metal case was elaborately engraved with a nautical scene: a mermaid lying belly-down on a rock, watching a tall ship sail away from her in the distance. He popped the case open and saw that the needle of the compass was pointing towards him. He didn't know how far he could be from home or whether they had already sailed east or west, but he knew they were now travelling south. England was definitely somewhere north of wherever he was now. He lay down in the bed once more and looked up through the porthole at the underside of a lifeboat: his lifeboat. He clicked the compass closed and slid it under the pillow and pulled out a brown and orange striped box embossed with the words *Beattie's Sweeties* in gold.

As you probably know, sometimes something happens that triggers a person's memory. Staring at the gilded letters, Ludlow felt as though he was about to remember something when the door to Raghnall's quarters creaked and inched slowly open again.

"Hello?" he asked, not seeing anyone there.

"It's...me," Harry called from the floor, panting. Ludlow pushed the door ajar just enough for her to fit through it and she hopped up onto the bed beside him, hugging a hunk of white bread.

"What do you want?" he asked.

"I brought you some bread," she said, dropping it at her

feet. "It's fairly fresh."

He picked it up and placed it on Raghnall's pillow. "Thanks," he said.

"Aren't you going to eat it?" she asked.

"I'm not hungry," he said. "Maybe later. So, what do you want?"

"I know you're planning something," she said. "You're going to take me with you."

"I'm not planning anything," he said.

"Of course you are," she said. "You must be, and if you're not, you should start planning something. Morag will never let you go. She'll never let either of us go. Take me with you," she said. "You can trust me."

"You kidnapped me and brought me on board this ship to save yourself."

"Look, Laszlo, you're what? Ten years old?" she asked.

"I think I'm eleven," he answered. "And it's Ludlow," he corrected her.

"Eleven years old and small for an eleven-year-old at that. You'll never escape on your own. It's too far to swim. There are the lifeboats, but have you ever rowed a boat before?"

"No," he said, and then without thinking he went on, "but *I* won't be rowing."

"I knew it. You *are* planning something."

CHAPTER 9

The plan had been hatched and all that remained was for Ludlow to await nightfall and the end of Raghnall's shift. He had debated the merits of bringing a forgetful, foul-smelling goblin with him for most of the morning, and finally decided he couldn't row a boat on his own—he hardly knew how—and especially for such a great distance. There was no choice but to recruit Raghnall for the journey, although it would have to wait until the last moment, when there was no chance of Raghnall accidentally revealing the plan.

Ludlow closed his eyes. He opened them again. He tossed in the bed. He turned in it. He slipped into sleep and out of it again, and finally gave up trying.

He lay in the bed listening to a cacophony of sounds: arguing and laughing, the wind catching the sails, the waves crashing against the ship's hull, and a creak of footsteps coming down the stairs. They weren't loud footsteps, but somehow Ludlow heard them over every other sound. He slowly pushed the door ajar and peered through the crack, and there was Morag, drifting past the rows of hammocks and counting them, one by one, once and again and then a third time.

"Twenty-one, twenty-two, the hammock of Raghnall makes twenty-three, and the hammock of the new one makes twenty-four," she said to herself. "There is only one berth left to fill." She stood before the last empty hammock and ran her long, translucent fingers delicately over the interlocked ropes.

Another interesting fact about banshees is that they are known to fixate. Being undead spirits and existing for much longer than the average human lifespan, and not having any family or friends, not having to go to school or work or having any responsibilities whatsoever, they have nothing but time on their hands to obsess. While there are any number of things in the world one could obsess about, one of the two popular obsessions among banshees is numbers.

"One more child," Morag said, "and then I will have a full ship's compliment, as they say."

She laughed an unnerving laugh before spinning on her heel back towards the staircase and prancing almost gleefully up the stairs. Though Ludlow's stomach had finally settled, her laugh and giddiness made him slightly queasy once more.

"One more child," he said.

Incidentally, the other popular obsession among banshees is revenge.

CHAPTER 10

Ludlow had finally fallen asleep only to be awoken by the pounding of a fist on the door to Raghnall's quarters and the horrible, nose-crinkling smell of goblin.

"Human!" the goblin shouted. "Human, we're all wanted on the upper deck. That means you as well."

"Why?" Ludlow asked through the door.

"Why what?" the goblin asked.

"Why are we wanted on the upper deck?" Ludlow asked.

There was a pause and then the goblin asked, "Who said that?"

"Never mind," Ludlow said, exasperated. "I'm coming."

He opened the door to see a startled goblin looking back at him.

"You're not Raghnall," the goblin said. "What're you doing in Raghnall's quarters?"

"Never mind that," Ludlow said, pushing his arms into the sleeves of his cardigan. "Why does Raghnall sleep in here? Why doesn't he sleep in his hammock?"

"Well, Morag lets him sleep in here because this is where we've stored all his things," he said. "He collects things, you see?"

"Steals things, you mean?" Ludlow asked.

"I think some of them're his. Anyway, the only thing you need to remember is no one else is allowed to sleep in Raghnall's hammock. Nobody is allowed to sleep in twenty-three. It's his hammock, whether he sleeps in it or not."

"I see," Ludlow said.

"See, my hammock is number nineteen," he said. "Only Sully can sleep in hammock nineteen."

"So, you're Sully," Ludlow said.

"Yes," Sully answered. "Who are you?"

Ludlow just shook his head and said, "Let's go then."

"Where?" Sully asked.

"To the upper deck. We're all wanted on the upper deck, remember?"

"Oh, right," he said, heading towards the stairs.

"So, why is it so important that no one sleeps in your

hammock?" Ludlow asked, following behind.

"I don't know," Sully said. "I don't know why anyone would want to sleep in my hammock anyway."

"Why shouldn't they?"

"Well, for one thing, it's full of holes."

CHAPTER 11

From the top of the stairs Ludlow could already see the mass of land on the horizon. Lush shades of green topped jagged, rocky cliffs, and the ruins of a sort of castle sat nestled on a lofty peak. It was like something out of a fairy tale, and he wondered if it was real.

"Where are we?" he asked, as Harry flew past him. "What is this place?"

Harry stopped just behind him and hovered at the eyepiece of a long brass telescope and looked through it, not answering.

"Is this one of the Channel Islands?" he wondered aloud, standing on the tips of his toes, trying to get a better view over the heads of the assembled goblins. Ludlow had been very good in geography at school, and the Channel Islands were, of course, detailed in Volume C of the *Encyclopaedia*

Britannica. "Maybe Jersey?" he asked.

"Have you come up with an escape plan yet?" Harry whispered, not turning her eyes away from the scope.

"I'm still working on it," he fibbed.

"Well, get on it. Quickly," she said.

"Adhair?" Morag called. "Do we have a location?"

"Yes, ma'am," Harry replied, and perched on the telescope.

"Good," Morag answered. "Goblins," she said, stepping onto a pedestal and towering above the crowd, "the time has come again."

Time for what? Ludlow wondered, as a grumble of voices rose from the horde of goblins in front of him, asking "What does she mean?" "What time did she say it was?" and the occasional comment, "Sorry, I don't have the time." Morag held one hand outstretched and examined her cracked fingernails.

"If you have finished with your inane questions," Morag said, as the crowd finally quieted, "I will answer them. We will drop anchor here and in a few hours, when darkness is almost upon us, Raghnall, Sully, Corcoran and Harry will go ashore to collect one more child."

While the goblins again grumbled amongst themselves, Ludlow looked to Harry. She was looking back at him, mouthing "quickly" once more. *Maybe it's time for a new plan*, Ludlow thought, and before he knew it the words "maybe I should go with them" were being spoken by someone at the back of the crowd and loudly.

"What did he say?" Morag shouted.

Ludlow was speechless. Though he couldn't make his mouth speak words at that moment, the ones going through his mind were *did I really just say that*?

"He said maybe he should go with us," Harry answered.

"Do you think me mad?" Morag asked.

"Don't answer that," Harry whispered.

"Why would I give my captive an opportunity to escape?" she asked. "I mean, my dear child, my son, why would I give you an opportunity to escape the bonds of my affection?"

Harry looked at Ludlow desperately until an idea finally came to him. It wasn't the worst idea he could have come up with, but it wasn't the best one either.

"Well, you need someone to keep an eye on Harry," he said. "She's dying to get off this ship. For good, I mean."

One goblin from the crowd piped up with a "that's true," while others nodded in agreement.

"If you send me, I'll make sure she doesn't get away," he said. His new plan was taking shape. He was becoming more and more convinced that he and Harry would be escaping the ship that night.

"Last time you told her you'd let her go when the job was done but you didn't," he went on. "She won't fall for that a second time."

"How do you know that? Did she tell you that?" Morag asked.

"It's true isn't it?" Ludlow asked.

"Yes," Morag answered. "So how do you propose to prevent a fairy from escaping?"

"Well, you could chain us together," he said.

"I do like that idea," Morag said, another crooked smile spreading across her chapped lips.

"Backstabbing two-timer," Harry muttered. It was only then that Ludlow looked over at her. If he had done so sooner maybe he would have stopped talking. Harry, apparently, did not like the idea. Harry was not smiling. In fact, Harry's lips were pursed and her entire face was as red and sour as a pickled beet, although Ludlow couldn't imagine why.

"It is decided then. Though it pains me to part with my dear child, the little beast will go ashore." Ludlow was still quite pleased with himself for all of one minute, until Morag said, "Corcoran, you will chain yourself to Harry and the boy so neither one of them can escape."

CHAPTER 12

Every time Corcoran took another stroke, the chains got partly tangled in the oars and Ludlow and Harry were jerked backwards and forwards until the goblins managed to untangle them.

"Why do you insist on rowing?" Harry finally asked, gripping the manacle that hugged her waist.

Creatures human beings don't believe in have varying personalities, like human beings themselves. Goblins especially. It's hard to tell because they all struggle so with memory loss, but when they aren't forgetting or arguing, they are actually quite different. Raghnall was clever and kind and could even be rather humorous, at times on purpose. Sully was a bit simple-minded and had a fear of dogs, though he probably couldn't remember if there was a good reason. Neither Sully nor Raghnall were unpleasant in any way, other than the distinct odor of goblin. Corcoran, on the other hand, was a brute. He was physically bigger and stronger than all the other goblins and frightfully stupid, as was evidenced by his continued attempts to row a boat with his arms chained to a fairy and a human child.

"Let Sully or Raghnall row," Harry said, but Corcoran dropped the oars into the water once more and again had to stop rowing to untangle them.

"I'm sorry about this," Ludlow said.

"What?" Harry shouted. It was almost impossible to hear each other over the clinking and jangling of the chains.

"I said 'I'm sorry!'" he shouted back as all went quiet again. The corner of Harry's mouth curled up in a half-smile.

Just as Corcoran was about to set the oars back down, they heard Morag shout, "Let Raghnall row, you fool!" They looked back to see that they hadn't even moved ten meters from the *Anathema* and that the entire crew was assembled along the ship's edge, watching them go nowhere fast.

"Oh, yes, ma'am," Corcoran said with an awkward salute, and moved back to let Raghnall take the oars.

"Remain calm," they heard Morag say. "Remain calm."

Though the sea was a bit choppy, it was still a much smoother journey from then on. Ludlow saw two children far off in the distance, playing alone on a sandy beach under the lowering sun. He worried the lifeboat might be heading their way, until it turned into a little bay lined with trees, with almost no beach to speak of and not a person in sight.

As they drew closer to the island, a strange purple bird flitted up to them and hovered near Ludlow. He had never had a bird come so close to him before, had never seen a bird such as this one and wouldn't see this one for much longer before it vanished into thin air.

"What was that?" Ludlow asked.

"A weejy weejy bird," Harry said.

There are a number of creatures in existence that are virtually unknown to humans and all for good reason. These are referred to as "Creatures Human Beings Have Never Heard Of." The weejy weejy bird is one such creature.

Its name is derived from the *weejy* sound it makes as it spins like a top, flapping its single wing and pivoting around its own body. It moves so quickly and disappears so suddenly that when a human does spot one, they usually think they're hallucinating.

"Where did it go?" Ludlow asked.

"No one knows where they go," she answered. "One minute they're here and the next, *poof*, they're gone," she said. "You were lucky just to see it before it vanished."

"Lucky," Ludlow said. "Right. It's my lucky day," he said, holding up his chained arm to remind her how unlucky it really was.

"Right," she said. "Sorry."

"Here comes another one," Raghnall said, looking off into the distance.

"I'll slow it down," Harry said, placing her fingertips on her temples.

Suddenly, everything slowed down for Ludlow: the rowing of the oars, the words that were being spoken around him and the movement of the weejy weejy bird as it approached the lifeboat. He watched it spin towards him in slow motion. Its back was red and its front was a glittering blue and, indeed, it had only one strong wing on one side that it flapped and flapped, until it seemed to disappear behind it, like a magician behind a cape.

After it vanished, time quickly caught up with him. Raghnall was rowing normally and Ludlow could understand what everyone was saying, though it was an argument among goblins about something they couldn't remember and wasn't worth overhearing anyway. As you may recall, Harry had the ability to alter human beings' perceptions of time.

"How did you do that?" Ludlow asked. "That was incredible."

"Incredible? Well," she said, "I can see why you'd think so, but I've conjured far more impressive illusions of time."

"More impressive than that?" Ludlow asked.

"Far more," she said again. "I once brought time almost to a full stop for an entire houseful of people."

"Really?" he asked, looking back out over the water.

"The time catches up eventually," she continued.

Ludlow looked every which way, hoping to spot another weejy weejy bird. What he didn't know is that they only ever appear two at a time, which is, incidentally, the reason for their duplicate name. He was so fascinated by the birds that he'd almost forgotten what they were doing, until...

"We've got some movement over there," Sully said, looking through a pair of rusty old binoculars. "Everybody quiet down."

"Better do your thing, Harry," Corcoran said.

Before Ludlow could finish asking what thing that was, he was sitting in a lifeboat with three unattractive teenaged boys and a girl and looking down at the hairy paws of an English sheepdog.

As you may recall, Harry had the ability to alter human beings' perceptions of creatures.

CHAPTER 13

The two unchained goblin-boys jumped clumsily from the lifeboat and pulled it mostly out of the water before tying it to a rotting tree stump. Corcoran lumbered out of the boat after them, dragging Harry and Ludlow along behind him through a narrow tract of forest and onto a paved road.

"Which way now, Harry?" Raghnall asked. Ludlow wouldn't have known it was Raghnall if he hadn't recognized his voice, of course, because Raghnall looked nothing like himself. He had been transformed into a gangly, curly-haired teenaged boy, dressed in a school uniform and trainers.

"Left," she answered. Harry looked just as she always did, only average human size, without wings, and wearing a similar uniform to Raghnall's and penny loafers. Ludlow looked down at where his feet should have been and again saw his fluffy grey paws.

"This is insane," he said, quite loudly.

"Shhh," Harry hushed. "Dogs don't speak English."

"Sorry," he said. "Can't you make my voice sound like a dog whimpering or something?"

"Of course I could," she answered, "but a whimpering dog would still attract attention anyway. Just be quiet."

Raghnall and Sully had slowed and now lagged a distance behind them. Sully cleared his throat. "Erm," he started.

"Shhh," Harry snapped back at him.

"What are we doing again?" Sully called.

"Shhh," Harry snapped again.

"A better question is 'are we really doing this?'" Ludlow whispered to her. He tried to keep a few paces back from Corcoran, but, though he couldn't see it anymore, the chain kept yanking him forward.

"What do you suggest?" she asked. "Thanks to you, we're chained to the biggest, oafiest goblin on the ship. We can't get away, and we can't go back to the ship empty-handed."

"Why not?" Ludlow asked.

"Morag would wail so hard you'd be lying ill on your back for days," she said. "Is that what you want?"

"Of course not."

"Then this is how it's got to be."

"Why does she want another child anyway?"

"She loves children. Now be quiet," Harry ordered.

Corcoran shushed them both and stopped behind a small old stone building and waited. He, Harry and Ludlow peered around the corner as the others finally caught up to them. The building, as it turned out, was a mausoleum at one end of a cemetery. Not the kind of dark, gloomy cemetery you'd read about in a ghost story. The sun shone through the trees onto freshly cut grass. Tombstones jutted out here and there; some were so old the letters weren't even visible from where they stood and wildflowers had been allowed to grow up high around them, and others were shiny and new. A family was gathered around one new tombstone in particular, listening to a vicar speak words Ludlow couldn't hear and dabbing at their eyes with tissues. Ludlow couldn't help but wonder at how strange this funeral seemed. He thought funerals only happened in the rain.

"There are three children," Harry whispered.

"What?" Ludlow asked, finally realizing what they were doing there. "Are you insane?"

"Should we take a vote on that?" Raghnall asked.

Ludlow probably should have wondered why Raghnall had asked that or why Raghnall hadn't forgotten what was even going on, but he was too preoccupied or, more accurately, gripped with fear at the realization of what they were about to do.

"Kidnap a child from a funeral?" Ludlow asked. "That's the plan?"

"It's the easiest way," Harry started. "The grief..."

"They're not having a bad enough day?" Ludlow continued. "They've lost a loved one and now they're going to be kidnapped by you?" he asked. "Not to mention, it's impossible. There must be twenty people standing around there," Ludlow said. "Do you think you can just snatch one of their children away, right from under their noses? I don't care if you look like human children, they won't let you run off with one of their kids."

"Calm down," Harry whispered, "and don't make

another sound. I mean it."

The vicar finished speaking and made the sign of the cross in front of himself. The mourners placed flowers on the ground and slowly filed out of the cemetery along a gravel path. One little ginger-haired girl stayed behind, picking up the flowers and stacking them neatly in a little bouquet beside the tombstone. She clung to a haggard looking teddy bear, holding it with its head buried in her neck as her tears dripped onto its matted fur. Ludlow's heart was breaking at the sight of her.

"This is our chance," Harry whispered.

Slowly the red-haired girl turned to follow the others.

"Now, Harry," Corcoran ordered.

Harry opened her mouth to speak, but it was Ludlow who made a sound. He barked. He barked like a rabid dog who had just had his paw run over by a bicycle wheel and been stung by a bee, and he took off running towards the little ginger-haired girl. Corcoran pulled him back, of course, but he had done what he'd set out to do. The girl went running towards her family, who were all turned and looking at the motley crew of goblin boys, a fairy girl and a slobbering English sheepdog.

CHAPTER 14

Banshees are not forgiving creatures. They're not generally impressed by lengthy apologies, clever *I'm sorry* greeting cards, flowers or even chocolates. They are not anyone's mum or nana or dear old auntie. Harry knew this. The goblins knew it too when they could remember it. By now, Ludlow knew it as well as they did. They hardly spoke for most of the journey back to the ship. The wheels in Ludlow's head were turning, trying to figure out what to tell Morag. It would be impossible to successfully lie with Raghnall, Sully and Corcoran barely able to remember the truth of what actually happened, never mind a lie.

"Done for," Harry suddenly said. "We're done for. Finished. Are you happy now?"

"Of course I'm not happy," Ludlow said, "but I'm not sorry either."

"Humph," Harry grumbled, trying to cross her tiny arms around the manacle. "You will be sorry," she said. "I haven't known you for very long, but I'll bet that's the stupidest thing you've ever done. Stupid human."

"I'm not stupid," he said.

"Aren't you? First you allow yourself to be kidnapped, then we have an opportunity to escape and instead you get us chained to this nincompoop." She jerked the chain attached to Corcoran, but he hardly seemed to notice. He was actually almost asleep with his snout buried in his bulging chest. "And now we're going back to the ship empty-handed and who knows what Morag'll do," she said. "Stupid human."

"If I'm so stupid, why are you expecting me to come up with a plan?" he asked.

"That's a good point," Raghnall said.

"What is?" Harry asked.

"What's what?" he asked back, looking confused.

Harry snickered.

"That was mean," Ludlow said.

"It's not my fault he has a terrible memory," she said.

"It's not *his* fault either," Ludlow said. "So, go on. Why

don't you come up with an escape plan? In fact, if you're so clever, how did you wind up a prisoner on that ship?" Ludlow asked.

"That's a good question," Sully said.

"If you must know, it was the lesser of two evils," she said.

"What does that mean?" Raghnall asked.

"It means being captive aboard the *Anathema* still beats being held captive by that wicked girl who trapped me in a jar and left me baking on her windowsill all day before she came home from school and tried to dissect me for her science class," she said. "Worse still was that power-hungry wizard who wanted me to help him become the prime minister. I couldn't let that happen. I do have a conscience, you know. Not to mention he fed me birdseed, the lout," she grumbled.

"Are you being serious?" Ludlow asked.

"Before them," Harry went on, "was that horrible, warty old witch who was obsessed with people seeing her as young and beautiful. I had to follow her everywhere she went and believe me, she went everywhere."

"Wait," Ludlow said, "If she was a witch, couldn't she

have just cast a spell to make herself young and beautiful?"

"Ludlow, just because you're a witch doesn't mean you're any good at it. She was terrible. She fed me birdseed too. The cheap stuff," Harry said. "What's more, she used to flick me, you know, with her forefinger," she said, making the gesture herself.

It's considered the height of bad manners to flick away a fairy. Just as an aside, you should also be aware that this rule doesn't apply only to fairies. It is the height of bad manners to flick any creature, under almost any circumstances.

"You're making all of this up, aren't you?" Raghnall asked.

Harry shrugged.

"Well, if you're so good at making up stories, why can't you figure out something to tell Morag?" Ludlow asked, as the ship loomed large ahead.

"I have thought of something," she answered.

"What?" he asked.

"The truth, of course," she answered.

"Good plan," Raghnall said.

"It's the only plan," Harry said. "We can't come up with a story, because you three thick heads won't remember it."

Raghnall and Sully looked at one another, blankly.

Harry shook her head.

"Wait," Ludlow said. "Raghnall, Sully, Corcoran, what happened back there?"

"What?" Sully asked. "Back on the island?"

"I remember a dog barking and a little girl running away," Raghnall said.

"Yes, there was a dog," Sully said. "I definitely remember hearing a dog. I'm afraid of dogs."

"What about you, Corcoran?" Ludlow asked, but Corcoran was now sound asleep.

"Hey, Corcoran!" Harry shouted, punching him in the shoulder with both fists. "What happened back there?"

Corcoran yawned and scratched his head for a minute and then said, "Well, we were about to snatch a little girl but then a dog barked and the whole plan went belly-up."

"So who's to blame for us not getting the girl then?" Ludlow asked.

They all agreed, "The dog is, of course."

"There you have it," Ludlow said to Harry.

"Brilliant," she said with a smile.

CHAPTER 15

Just as all fairies possess an individual gift, all banshees are cursed. You may be of the opinion that just being a banshee is curse enough, and you would be right, but nevertheless, each banshee possesses a unique curse that is hers alone. Morag was no different. Harry would have known this, but the exact nature of Morag's curse was a well-guarded secret from the entire crew of the *Anathema*, Harry included.

Four of the attempted kidnappers stood side by side on the quarterdeck like sailors standing at attention and one hovered in the air beside them while Morag paced back and forth in front of them, the lantern in her hand lighting their faces as she passed. No one had spoken, but it was glaringly obvious that they hadn't succeeded.

"Goblins," Morag finally said with a sigh. "What did I

ever do to deserve goblins?" she asked.

Perhaps they were all bright enough to know that she didn't actually expect an answer to that question, or perhaps three out of five of them had already forgotten what the question was. Either way, still no one spoke.

"So," she said, after another long pause, "five of you left to kidnap a child, and five of you returned without a child. I have counted your numbers again and again, and still there are only five of you when there ought to be six."

"There was a dog, ma'am," Ludlow said, his voice cracking and barely raising above a whisper.

"What was that?" Morag asked, stopping in front of him.

"There was a dog," he said, more clearly. "We were about to snatch a little girl, but a dog barked and scared her away."

"And then an entire funeral procession spotted us," Harry said. "It was too risky."

"Is this true, Raghnall?" Morag asked.

"Yes, ma'am," he answered. "A dog barked."

"Corcoran?" she asked.

"What?"

"Was there a dog?" she asked.

"Where?" he asked.

"Is there a dog about?" Sully asked. "I'm afraid of dogs."

"Shall I set a course for the Isle of Dogs, ma'am?" Raghnall asked.

"No!" she shrieked. "Confounded goblins! What did I ever do to deserve you?"

The water began to rise around them, the wind began to whistle through the sails, and by now you'll know what happened next: the banshee wailed.

CHAPTER 16

As previously mentioned, a banshee's wail can be provoked in two ways: (1) it can be caused by the banshee's sensitivity to the impending natural death of a human, or (2) it can be caused by a banshee's rage and can result in the death of the nearest human. Most banshees are benevolent, sensitive spirits who mourn the death of a human. Morag's wails, however, were most often caused by rage. It was a deep-seated, violent resentment caused by something that had happened long before she ever became the spirit we've come to know in this story. To make matters worse, whether she had intended to or not, she had surrounded herself with some of the most frustrating and infuriating creatures in all of creation.

The wailing struck Ludlow even more violently this time than it had the first. One minute he was perfectly fine and the next he was on all fours, flush with fever, dripping with sweat and vomiting into a bucket of dirty water. Moments after that, he was lying on the deck, flinching at the cold seawater-doused rags being pressed against his neck and forehead and hearing Morag's voice offering him more pills whose names she couldn't pronounce and telling Harry that she would keep sending them ashore until they brought back one more child. He slipped in and out of consciousness, grasping at bits of the conversations going on around him, hearing Harry tell a goblin to scoop more seawater and less crabs next time, and Morag telling Raghnall he'd be sleeping in hammock twenty-three because Ludlow would be sleeping in Raghnall's quarters; if Ludlow died during the night, Raghnall could have his quarters back.

CHAPTER 17

L udlow didn't die during the night. What's more, when he awoke the next morning he felt better than he had from the moment he'd set foot on the ship. After all, today was the day he would finally escape the *Anathema*.

He opened the porthole and looked out at the sea and the silhouettes of islands that grew smaller and smaller and fainter and fainter in the distance. He looked up at the underside of the lifeboat, still there waiting to be rowed off to England. He checked his pockets for the compass, the pocket telescope and the tube of matches. He struggled to unscrew the end of the metal cylinder, which had become quite rusted, and a dozen wooden matches flew out onto Raghnall's bed. Ludlow thought he heard someone coming down the stairs and hurried to collect the matches and put them back in the tube, but there was a sound of muffled voices from above and the footsteps faded up the stairs once more.

Ludlow sat waiting, anxiously. To avoid Morag and especially to avoid being sent on another kidnapping mission, he'd thought it best to fake sick and hide out in Raghnall's quarters for as long as possible. He laid down and sat up and laid down again. If you've ever pretended to be sick when you really weren't, you'll know that pretending to be sick and tired when you really aren't is dreadfully dull. So you can imagine that it is even harder to pretend to be sick when you are trying to plot an escape from a ship captained by a banshee and crewed by goblins.

He waited as long as he possibly could, which wasn't long at all, and finally inched open the door to Raghnall's quarters and peered out.

Past the rows of swinging hammocks, on the far right, was the staircase leading to the middle and upper decks, and on the far left was a door.

The storage room? he thought.

Ludlow didn't remember having seen a door in the storage room, but it had been quite dark, and he had only seen what Harry's light had shown him. He wondered now if the storage room was what was behind the door. *Even if it isn't*, he thought, *maybe there are more supplies in there I could use in my escape.*

He crept as quietly as he could across the lower deck. The planked wooden floor was shockingly creaky in certain places and slick with water in others, and when he wasn't causing a creak or gasping as he skidded along, he was batting away hammocks that swung into his face. He stopped now and then to listen for footsteps or voices approaching, but the crew were all safely busying themselves on the decks above.

The door wasn't latched but was so tight in the frame that Ludlow had to pull on it with both hands. It finally jerked open, sending Ludlow falling back onto his bottom and letting out a muffled "Ouf," but he was so relieved to have opened it—and that he didn't hear anyone coming down the stairs—that his sore bottom hardly bothered him at all.

The room was pitch dark within, but Ludlow was able to reach a lantern that hung from the rafters above him. He crept inside. Though the empty sacks had been replaced with flour-filled ones and the packing crates had been removed, it was, indeed, the storage room he'd been trapped in with Harry. Whether they had been there before or not, Ludlow now noticed glass jars on one shelf, containing something that might have been pickles at one time but were now so decomposed they could have been anything, next to the mysterious wooden barrels wrapped in rope. He grabbed the one remaining empty sack and a loaf of bread, but apart from those two things, there was nothing in the room that Ludlow could have used in his escape.

He turned around to leave and discovered another glass jar, a huge one, not with his eyes, but with one of his toes. If you've ever stubbed your toe before, you'll know that the cure for stubbing your toe is to close your eyes, shriek in pain, grit your teeth, grab the injured foot with both hands and hop around in a circle on the other. If you ever find yourself in a place you shouldn't be when this happens and you don't want to be found out, you should rather clap one hand over your mouth. Interestingly, all creatures who have toes instinctively use these techniques to treat this condition.

After dropping the sack of bread, shouting the word "Dammit!" into his hand and finishing his dance of agony,

Ludlow looked down at the jar. It was almost empty, but the glass was thick and heavy. Not only was it bigger than all the other jars in the storage room, it was also much newer looking. There was a metal lid on the top with holes punched into it and at the bottom there was a thin layer of what looked like garden soil and some twigs and dried crumbling leaves. He turned it around to reveal a faded white label that read *Kingdom: Animalia, Class: Aves?, Genus: Fairae, Species: Obnoxious*, written in purple ink.

"Obnoxious?" he was reading quietly aloud, when he heard soft footsteps coming down the staircase. He gently pulled the door shut, gathered the sack and bread loaf from where they had fallen on the floor, crouched behind the barrels, blew out the lantern and waited for the creature to open the door to Raghnall's quarters and discover he was missing. But it didn't. In fact, it opened the door to the storage room.

A hand wielding a lantern first appeared through the door and then the rest of Morag entered. Ludlow watched her from behind the barrels. She crept in quietly, looking back towards Raghnall's quarters as she closed the door behind her.

She placed the lantern on the floor and walked over to the barrels. She hopped up onto one and sat facing away from Ludlow as she ran her hands over the barrel tops and winding ropes and hummed quietly to herself. Ludlow thought this was bizarre, to say the least, but she was a banshee, after all, and by now he had learned that banshees do strange things, like kidnapping children and keeping them captive on old ships, offering them expired medicine, and wailing at the impending death of a stranger or causing a stranger's death themselves.

She sat there awhile, eventually breaking into a shriek-y little song. Ludlow couldn't make out most of the words, except for "twenty-five," "children" and "die," which seemed to repeat themselves quite often. She was still singing the song almost fifteen minutes later when she finally jumped down from the barrels, snatched up the lantern from the floor with one hand and sauntered out. He didn't hear her latch the door behind her, just the echo of her song as she moved across the lower deck. She finished with one final "die" as her footsteps faded. He thought this might have been the strangest and scariest thing that had happened yet, but she did love children. Didn't she?

CHAPTER 18

Just as Ludlow closed the door to Raghnall's quarters behind him again, the ship jolted to a halt. The paintings on the wall swung and banged against each other, and waves crashed against the side of the ship and splashed through the open porthole. He jumped up to pull it closed and saw the thing that explained the terrible, shrill creaking sound that vibrated through the wood of the ship. A rock. An enormous, jagged rock. The tip of a land mass just small enough not to sustain any life, but large enough to tear a terrific hole in the *Anathema*. There were panicked voices and scurrying footsteps on the decks above him, then one goblin, no two, no four goblins dropped down past the porthole onto the wet rocks.

"What happened?" one of them asked.

"Don't you remember, Bernie?" Raghnall asked.

"I'm sure I'll remember eventually, but right now I don't," Berneas answered.

"Don't what? What are we doing down here?" Raghnall asked.

What followed was a great deal of confusion, argument and questions that led them in circles and that they probably wouldn't remember anyway, until they finally turned back to face the ship.

"Corcoran, look at this hole!" Berneas said.

Ludlow couldn't see the damage himself, but he gathered from their discussions that the ship's hold was filling with water. There was no hope of it being repaired any time soon, but since the tides were on their way out, they'd surely be able to bail out the water and repair it by the time the waters began to rise again.

The tides, he thought.

Ludlow's plan would require a bit of tweaking now. He had no idea of when the tides would rise again, and would somehow have to find out whether he could make his escape that night as he had hoped. He eavesdropped on their conversation awhile longer, until an argument broke out over who had been steering the ship. No one could remember, but whomever it was, they were very cross with him, and they were still cross with him when Ludlow emerged from the lower deck and spotted Harry perched on the railing.

"We've run aground," she said, as he stopped beside her and looked out over the mass of rocks jutting up from the sea.

"On another island?" he asked, watching the rest of the goblins—he counted nearly twenty of them—drop one by one from the quarterdeck, the lucky ones landing safely on the slick rocks and the unlucky ones sliding immediately off of them into the water.

"I suppose it's an island, yes," she answered.

"At least there aren't any children on this one," he said.

"Of course there aren't," she said. "Look at it. It's just a pile of rocks. Not to mention most of it's underwater at high tide."

"How did I end up in the water?" they heard a goblin ask below.

"Where's Morag?" Ludlow asked, burying his hands in his pockets and clutching the compass.

"I don't know," Harry said. "Probably back in her

quarters trying to 'remain calm,' as she says. These goblins can be so insufferable at times that if she watched them at work she'd just wail for hours. If we were close enough to a village or town, she'd wipe out every person in it watching this crew handling an emergency," she explained, as another goblin found himself on his bottom in the water and asked how he had got there. "You'd be back in bed, that's for sure."

"So what's a banshee doing sailing with a crew of goblins if it's so, what you said?" he asked.

"Insufferable? Well, can you imagine her finding a crew of adult humans to do it? She'd kill at least one of them every time she got upset, but that's beside the point since they'd all go running at the mere sight of her and never join the crew in the first place."

"True," Ludlow said, and then something occurred to him. "Aren't there any other mythological creatures she could have hired for the job?"

"Mythological creatures? You mean creatures human beings don't believe in but exist just the same?" she asked. "There are no mythological creatures. Mermaids, trolls, elves, unicorns—all real."

"Okay, then couldn't she have hired some other creatures human beings don't believe in?" Ludlow asked.

"She didn't hire them. They were already here when she came aboard. Once she caught onto their trouble with memory, she just started acting like she was the captain and none of them remembered that she wasn't."

"Why didn't you tell them?" he asked.

"I wasn't here," she answered.

"Then how do you know what happened?"

"She told me," she said, grinning. "I tricked it out of her."

"How do you know she told you the truth?" Ludlow asked.

"You think she could con me?" Harry asked, the grin replaced with a look of disbelief. "Never."

"Well, why don't you tell them now then? Maybe they could do something to get rid of her," he said.

"I told them once, and there was a plan," she answered. Her voice slowly raised, "but just like everything else, they forgot it," she continued, before their conversation was completely interrupted by an incessant splashing sound from below. They watched as Raghnall sloshed back and forth through pools of shallow water, dragging broken planks of wood to higher ground.

"What do you think of Raghnall?" Ludlow asked when he seemed to be finished.

"Well, he's alright as far as goblins go, I suppose. He doesn't really fit in with the rest of them. He likes art and reading fiction and other human things. He's quite intelligent too."

"Intelligent? He forgets a question you asked him only seconds earlier," Ludlow said.

"What does being forgetful have to do with being intelligent?" she asked. "Besides, they often remember eventually. Except arguments—they'll argue with each other for years and never remember why. They only remember that they're cross with each other."

As if to prove her point, Raghnall took out a measuring tape and a slightly damp notepad and pencil and started drawing up plans to repair the hull of the ship, while Sully unpacked a satchel of hand tools and yelled about how cross he was with him for no apparent reason.

"Curious creatures," Ludlow said.

The work to repair the ship had gotten underway quite

quickly. Say what you will about goblins, but they are hard and efficient workers once they remember what they're supposed to be doing, especially if they aren't distracted by questions that turn into tedious conversations. It was barely tea time when the last pail of water was tossed out and the last dollop of tar was slapped onto the hull, but the ship itself sat grounded on a never-ending beach. The sea had retreated nearly out of view by the time the work was finished, giving Ludlow time to wander the upper deck and quarterdeck and work out the details of his escape.

There were four lifeboats, enough for the whole crew— especially with most goblins being not quite the size of an average person. It occurred to Ludlow for the first time that also meant there were enough lifeboats for the entire crew to pursue him. Even though the ship was grounded, if he could get away in a lifeboat, they could come after him in the other lifeboats. He would just have to hold out hope that they wouldn't wake up or notice he was missing until he and Raghnall were well away—possibly with Harry in tow, although he wasn't yet decided on that point.

Ludlow was right to be wary of her. Fairies are beautiful creatures to the human eye, delicate, dainty and radiant, but their beauty is often their only redeeming feature. They are not known for their loyalty. When it comes down to it, a fairy will almost never put another creature's well-being ahead of its own. They are immeasurably selfish. Even fairies that don't possess Harry's power to enchant humans use other methods of trickery and deceit to get their way. All creatures human beings don't believe in know this, so Harry wouldn't have been well liked by anyone aboard the *Anathema*, which is probably why she answered so many of Ludlow's questions and had even begun to seek him out for company: (1) it must be quite lonely to be a fairy; and (2) she thought he could do something for her, like help her escape.

The prospect of escaping definitely wasn't far from her mind when she found him on the upper deck later that evening.

"They'll be serving supper soon," she said, as she settled on his shoulder.

"Good. I'm starving. I've only had a bit of bread and water for two days now," he said.

"Well, you're in for a treat then," she said. "Slop is on the menu tonight."

"Slop? Sounds tasty."

"Don't humans eat slop?"

"What is it?"

"It's slop. You know? Flour and water," she explained.

"So, it's paste," he said.

"Yes. Have you ever tried it?"

"Only to glue things together with," he answered. "I used it to make a mask in art class."

"To eat?" she asked.

"No, of course not," he answered, frustrated. "Why don't they just eat fish?"

"Ugh," she replied. Her face twisted and her tongue spilled out of her mouth. "That's disgusting." When her face recovered from the apparently horrifying suggestion she asked, "Aren't you going to come and eat?"

"No, thanks. I'll pass. I'm just watching the sun set," he answered, hoping she wouldn't notice Raghnall down below collecting tools that had been forgotten on the beach. It was so quiet, though, that it was impossible not to hear him grunting and mumbling to himself as he shuffled about.

"And watching a lifeboat," she said, "and a goblin just

the right size to help you row one back to England."

"Do you reckon?" he asked.

"You're escaping tonight, aren't you?" she asked. She was no longer perched on his shoulder but was hovering in the air within an inch of the tip of his nose. When he looked at her, his eyes crossed. When he turned away, she followed, stalking him along the deck of the ship. "Are you taking me with you? I'm begging you. No, I'm ordering you. As your kidnapper I order you to take me with you."

"Do you know how ridiculous that sounds?" he asked.

"Harry," Corcoran called from the doorway of Morag's cabin. "You're wanted in the captain's quarters."

She gave Ludlow an uncertain look. "Coming," she answered.

What was that look? he wondered. Was it more pleading to take her with him or a threat not to cross her? Was she telling Morag that he had a plan to escape? He was so concerned about what Harry might be telling Morag that he didn't notice Raghnall had climbed back onto the deck until he passed him by, his arms piled high with hand tools.

"Raghnall," Ludlow called.

"Oh," Raghnall replied, startled. He dropped the tools

onto the deck and was bending down to collect them again as he cheerily said, "hello."

"Hello. Listen, I was wondering if you could tell me when the tide will be high enough to get away from here in one of these lifeboats?"

"Oh, it'll be a few hours from now, human," he answered.

"What time is it now?" he asked, patting his pockets with his free hand. "Where's my pocket watch?"

"I think it's about six o'clock," Ludlow answered.

"What was I looking for?" Raghnall asked.

"Never mind that, Raghnall," Ludlow said. "How long until the tide is high enough for the ship to set sail again?"

"Oh, late tonight," he answered as he bent down to pick up the last of his tools. "Round about midnight, I'd say."

"Good, good. You're probably wondering why I asked you that, aren't you Raghnall?" he asked, noticing that Raghnall hadn't picked up his hand drill.

"Asked me what?"

"Nothing," Ludlow said, smiling. "Nothing at all."

CHAPTER 19

There are two extremely unpleasant things which couldn't be avoided for long periods of time when travelling aboard the *Anathema*. The first was running into Morag, which was a great pity because without the threat of her wailing at any moment and making him violently ill or killing a passing stranger accidentally or on purpose, Ludlow might have enjoyed his time aboard. He stood on the quarterdeck of the ship, looking out at the glistening rocks and tidal pools that flashed with silvery shells and green seaweed. The sea stretched out to the horizon and the pink setting sun. He marvelled at the beauty of it all. The racket of clinking dishes and dragged tables and chairs on the middle deck was muffled by the closed hatch, so the only sounds Ludlow really noticed were the distant waves of the slowly rising sea. With the hatch also containing the foul smell of the crew, he was even inspired to take in a lungful of the crisp evening air before he got back to what he had been doing.

What had he been doing, you ask? Morag seemed to be wondering the same thing.

"You there, Twenty-four!" she shouted across the deck. "What are you doing there?"

He jerked upright and hurriedly stuffed something into his belt and pulled his cardigan closed around him.

"I asked you a question," Morag said, as she approached.

He turned to face her. "I...didn't know you were speaking to me," he answered.

"What are you up to, you horrible little beast?" she asked. "What have you got there?" She reached out to touch the lump in his side.

"Nothing," he said, flinching away from her. It jabbed him as he moved and he couldn't help but wince.

She stepped back, a look of surprise on her face which surprisingly turned to a look of grave concern.

"Are you ill?" she asked.

"No," he answered. He looked down and spotted three long coils of wood shavings at his feet. "I mean yes!" he shouted. "Yes, I feel ill," he said, quickly trotting down the stairs and towards the hatch with Morag close behind him.

"Do you need medicine?" she asked.

"No," he said, trying to pull the hatch open with one hand and hold his cardigan closed with the other.

"Are you hungry then?" she asked. "You have only had bread and water since you joined us. Children are usually ravenous little beasts, are they not?"

"I thought you...loved children," Ludlow said, still pulling.

"I do," she answered, unconvincingly.

"Well," he said, "I've never had anyone call me a beast before...and especially not a horrible one," he said, panting. "And I don't know what *ravenous* means, but it doesn't sound good."

"*Ravenous* simply means 'exceedingly hungry,'" she said.

"Oh," he replied.

"And *beast* is what I called my son," she said.

Ludlow stopped pulling and stared at her.

"Yes, I had a son," she said.

A banshee child? Ludlow thought. Was there such a

thing?

"I was taken away from him too soon," she said. "I believe they named him James."

"Oh, I'm sorry," Ludlow said. "You must miss him terribly."

"Terrible," she said, staring off into the distance.

"No. I said 'terribly,'" he said.

"Terrible," she repeated.

Neither of them said anything for a few moments as Morag seemed to be lost in thought and Ludlow couldn't think of anything else to say. They stood in uncomfortable silence until...

"What were we talking about?" Morag asked.

"I don't remember," Ludlow said, and it was true. He didn't.

"You do not remember?" Her brow furrowed and a look of concern spread across her face once more. "Are you sure you do not need medicine?" she asked, leaning down and grabbing his arms. "I have medicine in my quarters. Do you remember the medicine in my quarters?"

"Yes," Ludlow answered.

"Yes, you need medicine?" she asked, staring into each

of his eyes as if she was looking for something.

"No, I remember the medicine, but I don't need any, I promise. I'm probably just..." Ludlow started, but couldn't bear to finish. He closed his eyes and squinted them in disgust.

The second extremely unpleasant thing which couldn't be avoided for long periods of time when travelling aboard the *Anathema* was eating slop.

"Hungry?" she asked, and, unwillingly, Ludlow nodded.

"Then you shall have all the slop your beastly little heart desires," she said, and reached down to pull open the hatch.

The goblins all seemed surprised at the sight of Ludlow on the stairs, but after a "Who's that then?" and a "He's not getting any of my slop" and an "Oh, it's just that human," they all quickly went back to the business of slurping up their bowls of paste.

"Raghnall," Morag called from behind Ludlow, "get the human child a bowl of slop."

Raghnall scurried off into a room Ludlow hadn't been into yet, which he assumed must be the galley, and brought back a clean empty bowl and a glass of fresh water. He set them down on the long table and then took his seat on the bench once more.

"Go," Morag said, and Ludlow, unable to think of a way out of it, went.

He sat down on the bench next to Raghnall and pulled the glass of water towards himself as another goblin scooped a ladleful of slop into the empty bowl and shoved it at him.

He sat looking down at it for some time. He looked up to see that Morag was still watching. He took a sip of water. He picked up a dirty napkin and wiped his sweaty brow with it. He took another sip of water. He looked around the table at the goblins' bowls, and wished he hadn't. Their bowls were filthy. The fresh slop had clearly been poured into them before they'd been properly cleaned from the last meal. On some he could actually see mould around the rims, others bore hardened spills of old slop caked onto the outsides and some were a combination of mould and spills. His own bowl, though, looked brand new. He lifted it up and looked at the outside and could see his warped reflection in the pristine glaze.

"Is there a problem, Twenty-four?" Morag asked.

"No," he said, putting the bowl back down onto the table.

He stared into the lumpy white mush.

"This isn't paste," he told himself quietly. "This is a shepherd's pie, the way Nana makes it, with garlic and spring onion mash and diced carrots mixed in with the corn," he said. He looked back at Morag, who was still eying him with suspicion, and then spotted Harry a few seats over, sitting cross-legged on the table with a slop-caked soup spoon across her lap, watching him too. Then he noticed that most of the goblins were watching him.

"Are you going to eat that?" one finally asked.

"The secret ingredient to her shepherd's pie is fresh rosemary," Ludlow went on. "Lots of it. In the beef mixture," he said, as he scooped a spoonful of the thick paste into his mouth.

It tasted even worse than he had imagined. He thought it might have been made with vinegar rather than water. Then he remembered the jars of rancid something-or-other from the storage room and wondered if it had made its way into the recipe. He nearly choked on it as he heard a goblin ask what rosemary was, and another goblin ask who Rosemary was, and then, suddenly, he couldn't make out a single word of the inane conversation that went on around him. The words were being spoken so quickly that he couldn't decipher a single one. Then he heard, "An herb. I think it's an herb, used in cooking. Is that right, human?" a goblin was asking him.

He looked down into his empty bowl and up at the goblin who was speaking to him.

"Who's Herb?" another goblin asked. "Rosemary's brother?"

"Where did the slop go?" Ludlow asked, but as he spoke, he could taste it and as he licked his lips, he realized it was all over his mouth and chin.

"You ate it," Harry said, smiling at him.

"Don't you remember?" Raghnall asked, collecting Ludlow's dishes from the table.

"No," Ludlow said, realizing what Harry had done. "Thankfully, I don't."

"He's losing it," one goblin said, to which another goblin, of course, replied,

"Losing what?"

CHAPTER 20

Ludlow jumped at the sight of Raghnall in the doorway to his quarters, but Raghnall jumped higher. He'd obviously forgotten Ludlow was sleeping in his quarters, and possibly had forgotten who Ludlow even was in the first place.

"Raghnall," Ludlow said, clutching his chest, "you startled me."

Raghnall clutched his own chest harder, gasping, until a look of recognition came over his hairy face.

"Oh, right," he said. "I'll sleep in hammock twenty-three."

"No, stay," Ludlow said. "There's room for both of us." He shuffled back into a corner to make room.

"Alright then," Raghnall said, closing the door behind him.

"Is your shift over?" Ludlow asked.

"Yes, human. Day's over," he grumbled cheerily. "Must get to sleep now. Tomorrow's another day." He pulled his glasses from his face, folded them and placed them on the shelf next to his books.

"Raghnall, I'm leaving the ship tonight and I'd like you to come with me," Ludlow said quietly.

"Leave? The ship? How?" he asked.

"On a lifeboat," Ludlow answered.

"Oh, I see," Raghnall said, pulling the topmost blanket over himself. "Well, that's the best way, I suppose. Good night."

"Yes, but you *are* coming with me, right?" Ludlow asked.

Silence.

"Raghnall?"

Snoring.

Goblins snore something terrible. They are prone to respiratory infections because of the shape of their snouts: short and blunt. Luckily for Ludlow he was trying to stay awake, so Raghnall's snoring didn't bother him too much. He stood and looked out the porthole, up at the full moon and down at the moon's reflection in the rising water, then sat back down in the corner and waited.

After what seemed an age, but was probably only a few minutes of sitting in the dimly lit room watching his roommate sleep and listening to him snore, Ludlow pulled one of the books from the shelf, turned the knob on the oil lamp to raise the wick and opened up *Alice's Adventures in Wonderland*. In the light of the lamp, a gold book plate on the inside cover caught Ludlow's eye.

"A Gift to Penzance Library, Cornwall," he read aloud. "Penzance Library?" he asked. "He must have stolen it."

CHAPTER 21

Ludlow read the first two paragraphs, then flipped through the pages, stopping on each illustration before flipping forward again. When he got to the end, he started over. He stopped halfway through and put the book down. He stood up and looked through the porthole. The water had risen ever so slightly. He sat back down. He flipped through the book. He stood up. Looked out the window. Sat. Flipped. Stood. Looked. Sat. Over and over until the water had finally risen above most of the rocks.

He tried to nudge Raghnall out of sleep. He tried to shake him awake.

"Raghnall," he whispered. Then "Raghnall," he said. "Raghnall!" he almost shouted and the goblin's eyes slowly opened at last.

"Is it morning?" Raghnall asked. "What's going on?"

Ludlow opened his mouth to answer but didn't get the chance to.

"You're going to leave the ship," Raghnall suddenly remembered.

"Yes, exactly right, Raghnall, and I'm taking you with me," Ludlow said.

"Where are we going?"

"To England," Ludlow answered. He handed Raghnall his glasses and the burlap sack, empty but for a half-eaten loaf of bread, before returning to look out the porthole. "The water's risen enough for us to lower one of the lifeboats now," he continued, as Raghnall buttoned the top of his shirt and ran his fingers through the hair on his head and face like a comb. "Grab some spare clothes and get them in that sack."

"These are my only clothes," Raghnall answered, which shed some light on why goblins smelled so bad.

"Well then, let's just go," Ludlow said, moving towards the door.

"But my paintings, my books, I can't leave them here," Raghnall said.

"They're only things, Raghnall," he said.

"But they're all I have," he answered. Ludlow was so moved by the sadness in Raghnall's voice and the distraught look on his face that, against his better judgement, he began to take down the paintings, one by one, which, though small enough to fit into the burlap sack, made one terrible racket when the frames clinked against each other. The only things that made more noise than the frames were the metal bells on the alarm clock. The books were quite heavy, but there were only three of them: *Alice's Adventures in Wonderland*, *Peter Pan*, and *The Lion, the Witch and the Wardrobe*, so Ludlow packed them too, along with the chocolates, of course.

"Wait," Raghnall said. "What are you doing with my things?"

Ludlow dropped the sack onto the bed and grabbed Raghnall by the shoulders. "Raghnall," he said, "listen to me. This is very important. I need you to focus as hard as you can on not forgetting what I say or what we're doing, just until we're away from the ship. Can you do that?"

"I'll try, human," he answered.

"You do want to leave here, don't you?" Ludlow asked.

"Yes, human," he said. He seemed to be thinking it

through for a moment, and then, with more conviction, he nodded. "Yes. Very much."

Ludlow smiled and nodded back before dimming the lamp and making his way to the door. He leaned against it to listen for any sounds outside and, when he was satisfied that there was no danger, he slowly turned the knob and pushed the door open to peek out.

"Human?" Raghnall asked, and Ludlow jerked the door shut.

"What?" Ludlow asked.

"When we get to England, can we go to the National Portrait Gallery?" he asked.

At that moment, Ludlow probably should have wondered how Raghnall even knew what the National Portrait Gallery was, but he was too concerned about waking the other goblins or, even worse, Morag hearing them.

"Yes, Raghnall," he answered. "I promise. Now let's be very quiet."

What Ludlow didn't know is that goblins in general, not just Raghnall, are the soundest sleepers of all mythological creatures (that is to say, creatures human beings don't believe in). He would have had to knock over a rack of pots and pans or drop a bag filled with picture frames and a metal alarm clock for a goblin to even open one eye. The only creature he needed beware of waking was Harry, but he had already decided that Harry had to be awoken and brought with them, even if only to enchant anyone who came across a boy and a goblin in a lifeboat.

They crept past the snoring goblins and up the two flights of rickety stairs, lifted the hatch and peered out onto the upper deck and quarterdeck. They were completely deserted, but through the grimy windows of the captain's quarters they could see the faint glow of Morag pacing within. Ludlow dropped back down and sat on a step, trembling. He'd almost forgotten how frightening she could be and how frightened he should be of her.

"What are you doing?" Raghnall whispered down to him.

"If she catches us, she'll kill me," he whispered back.

"Well then, we should stay," Raghnall said, slowly lowering the hatch, until, "Human," he said, "I think you're in danger either way."

A little tear formed in the corner of Ludlow's eye and he could feel his nose starting to twitch. "I think you're right," he said.

They climbed through the hatch onto the upper deck, then the quarterdeck, crawled almost on their bellies past Morag's cabin and sneaked up the stairs to the poop deck and Harry's cage. Her empty cage. Ludlow scanned the decks for Harry's glow, from the stern of the ship to the bow, but didn't see it until he finally gave up looking and he and Raghnall made for the lifeboat. There she was, perched on the handle of an oar, waiting for them.

"I was looking for you," he whispered.

"Well, here I am," she answered.

"Harry's coming with us?" Raghnall asked, setting the burlap sack down on the deck.

"Yes," Ludlow said. "We need her."

"I suppose we do, but we'd be better off if we didn't," he grumbled, just loud enough for Ludlow to hear and Harry not to. "Harry's coming with us?" he asked again. "Yes. Sorry. I forgot. I remember now."

"Well done, Raghnall," Ludlow whispered.

They climbed into the lifeboat, and after Raghnall had gone through his list of safety precautions using Harry as a torch, and seemed satisfied that he had conducted all of his checks and had all of the standard supplies, he actually remembered something.

"My things," he said.

"What are you doing?" Ludlow whispered as Raghnall climbed back out of the lifeboat.

"I need my things," Raghnall said, gently picking up the burlap sack. "I almost left them behind."

"Quickly," Harry said.

"Quietly," Ludlow said, just as the bag slipped from Raghnall's hands and landed with a *clack* and *clatter* on the deck. By a stroke of luck, the crashing sound didn't awake the crew. Unfortunately, the heart-stopping clanging of the alarm clock bells did. The ringing resounded through the ship and it wasn't long before the first of the goblin crew climbed through the hatch.

Raghnall had tossed the sack into the lifeboat and climbed back in himself by the time the rest of the crew emerged and was already helping Ludlow to lower the dinghy into the shallow water.

"I haven't moved so quickly in as long as I can remember," Raghnall said, panting. Although as long as a goblin could remember wasn't actually that long at all.

"Hurry!" Harry shouted. She climbed into the burlap sack and finally stopped the alarm clock, but the damage had been done.

"Raghnall?" a goblin asked from above them. "Where are you going?"

"Are we leaving the ship?" Sully asked.

"Nobody," they heard Morag say, "is leaving this ship." Her voice was unusually calm and composed. She wasn't wailing, as they'd come to expect, or shouting; nor did she sound even the slightest bit distressed. They touched down on the surface of the water and as Raghnall untied the lifeboat from the ship, Morag finally appeared at the railing and looked down at them, the full moon glowing brightly behind and through her.

"Did you hear me?" she asked. "I said 'nobody is leaving this ship.'"

"You're wrong," Ludlow said, a tremor in his voice. He and Raghnall picked up the oars and used them to push off from the ship's hull. "We're leaving."

"Since I love children, even you," she said, "I will give you a chance to give up this pathetic escape attempt. If you come back now, I promise no harm will come to you."

"No, thank you," Ludlow said.

"Yes," Raghnall said, as he sat down and began to row away. "No, thank you."

"Did you hear that, Morag?" Harry asked. "No, thank you. Ha!" Then quietly to Ludlow she said, "She's going to send every one of those goons after us any minute now."

"Goblins, to the lifeboats!" Morag shouted. "Bring them back. I will be in my quarters."

As they rowed, they watched and listened to the goblin crew piling into the lifeboats on either side of the ship and arguing and shouting about whose turn it was to row. Then, as the boats lowered, they heard a chorus of "What are we doing?" "Why are we leaving the ship in the middle of the night?" "Look at that big patch in the hull!" and one solo "Why is the water so far away?"

"Maybe they'll forget what they're supposed to be doing," Harry said. She sat on the rudder, watching intently as they all were.

"It doesn't matter if they do," Ludlow said.

"Why not?" Harry asked.

"What's happening?" Raghnall asked, as the first boat landed on the water and the goblins all started jumping about in it.

"I'm wet," one said.

"A leak!" another one shouted. "Two leaks! Threeee leeeeeaks!"

"So many leaks!" Sully shouted as he grabbed onto the ropes and tried to climb back up to the deck. The other goblins stood in the boat, scooping the water out with their hands, a bucket, a cap and a boot, until the boat sank completely and they were forced to swim back to the rocks.

"Well, that's a bit of luck," Harry said, as the port side of the ship came into view.

"Very lucky," Raghnall said, as the second lifeboat touched down onto the water, and the whole scene repeated itself. As they watched the third lifeboat sink into the shallow sea, leaving the last of the dazed and confused goblins clinging to the rocks and trying to climb the ropes back up to the quarterdeck, Ludlow was feeling quite proud of himself.

"I don't understand it," Raghnall said. "I checked those boats only yesterday. I'm almost certain."

"Ludlow," Harry said, "you're pretty clever, for a human."

"Thanks," he said.

"Why isn't this boat leaking, I wonder?" Raghnall asked. He had stopped rowing and was bent down, inspecting the hull of the lifeboat.

"He sabotaged the other lifeboats," Harry said.

"There's nothing wrong with this boat, Raghnall, and those other boats were in perfect condition yesterday," Ludlow said, opening his cardigan and revealing the hand drill still looped into his belt.

"Oh," Raghnall said. "I see. Oh, well done, human. Well done."

"Thanks," Ludlow said.

"For what?" Raghnall asked.

"Never mind," he answered.

They kept watching the ship, even when the moon periodically disappeared behind clouds and all that could be seen were a few lanterns and the glimmer of Morag drifting past the windows of her quarters. If she looked out, she would spot them, and even if she didn't, it was only a matter of time before one of the goblins reached the quarterdeck and told her what had happened, if they could remember. Apart from wailing, though, there was nothing she could do about it now, not until high tide, but Ludlow was still worried.

"We should do everything we can to keep her from tracking us," Ludlow said.

"Agreed," Harry said.

"That means we have to move quickly and quietly," he said. The sounds of arguing goblins still carried across the water and he suspected their own voices might carry just as far.

"Agreed," Harry whispered.

"And no light," Ludlow said opening his cardigan again.

"Agreed," she huffed. She climbed into his shirt pocket, and as he pulled his cardigan closed around them the light went out.

CHAPTER 22

L udlow had spent many a rainy day poring over the maps in his encyclopaedias and geography books, and he was convinced that if they just travelled north he would eventually reach some part of England. So, northwards they rowed, away from the marooned ship, with Ludlow looking back every few moments until the ship had completely disappeared from view.

"Can we speak now?" Raghnall asked.

"Yes," Ludlow said. "Yes, what did you want to say?"

"Nothing," Raghnall said. "Anything. The quiet is becoming unbearable."

"I have a question," Harry mumbled. Ludlow unbuttoned his cardigan and she flew out into the open, coughing. "Whose cockamamie idea was this, anyway?" she asked.

"You wanted to escape. You escaped," Ludlow said.

"I didn't realize that was going to require spending half the night in your armpit," she said. "And look around. We're in the middle of nowhere. The sea is getting rougher and rougher by the minute. I'm probably going to meet a horrible death by drowning if I don't die of thirst or exposure or get picked off by some predatory bird first."

"Predatory bird?" he asked.

"Yes, birds that eat small animals and can't tell that I'm not one," she said.

"Look, I'm only eleven years old, okay? If you had a better idea, you could have shared it."

"I *did* have a better idea," she said.

"What was it?"

"It's no use crying over spilled milk," she said, arms crossed. "Let's just make the best of it."

"Why is the sea so choppy, I wonder?" Raghnall asked.

Ludlow and Harry looked at him, and then at each other, and then back at Raghnall, blankly.

"Well, no other vessels have passed us," he explained, "and there's no wind, but Harry's right. The sea is quite choppy. It's just strange."

"What could that mean?" Ludlow asked, just as something slapped against the side of the boat. "What was that?" he asked, picturing every kind of sea creature he could remember from science class and his encyclopaedias, and then imagining every kind of sea creature he'd ever read about in a story book.

Harry and Raghnall looked as confused as Ludlow did until the creature's shimmering tail flicked out of the water.

"Ugh, mermaids," Harry said.

Mermaids as a species are often misunderstood by humans. Some believe them to be good, as they are depicted in fairy tales, and some, such as sailors and fishermen, have believed them for centuries to be omens of shipwrecks and death. Luckily for Ludlow, this was not the case.

Unlike some other creatures, there is no characteristic or personality trait such as forgetfulness or selfishness that each mermaid has in common. One thing that all mermaids do have in common is that they hate to be called "fish-face," but one can hardly consider that a personality trait.

"Mermaids?" Ludlow repeated.

"I told you mermaids existed," Harry said.

"I know you did. I believed you. But how can it be? How can it be that in the whole eleven years of my life I've never once laid eyes on a single mytho..." Ludlow began, but at the sight of Harry's raised eyebrow he defended himself. "You know, there's a reason we call you mythological. We can't see you, so we think you don't exist. So why am I seeing so many of you all of a sudden?"

"And what would human beings do with us if they could see us?" she asked, arms still crossed in front of her.

Ludlow didn't know what to say. It didn't matter much, though, because at that same moment the mermaid he couldn't believe existed jumped out of the sea and tried to tip them into it.

Raghnall grabbed an oar and tried to push her off. Ludlow grabbed the other and tried to help him, while Harry tried to pull her away by her hair.

"Stop it," the mermaid cried. "I only want you to come

into the water."

"Why?" Harry asked.

"Why not?" she asked.

"We'll drown. We're not all swimmers, you know," Harry said, still pulling.

"Oh." The mermaid seemed confused by this revelation and instantly let go her grip on the edge of the boat. She slipped quickly back into the water and sank below the surface with Harry tangled in her hair. Ludlow and Raghnall watched helplessly as Harry's light disappeared into the depths of the sea. They sat back down and looked at one another, stunned and speechless, until she came spewing out of the water and flopped onto the floor of the lifeboat like a wet fish.

"Harry!" Ludlow squealed. He picked her up and held her to his chest while she coughed and spurted into his shoulder.

"That was unpleasant," she said, with a final cough.

"Where did she go?" Raghnall asked, looking overboard once more.

"Who cares? She almost killed me," Harry said, squirming out of Ludlow's hands and climbing back onto his shoulder.

"She wasn't trying to kill you, I'm almost sure," Ludlow said.

"She deliberately ensnared me in her hair," Harry said.

"You can't control your hair," Ludlow said, and then a thought occurred. "Can mermaids control their hair?"

Raghnall shook his head, but Harry went on for some time about how she had known many mermaids to manipulate their own hair to grab onto things. Raghnall shook his head again when she appeared to be finished, but then she went on about it some more.

"Couldn't a mermaid have helped us?" Ludlow finally suggested. It was something he had thought of almost immediately upon realizing he was face to face with a mermaid but hadn't had a chance to say until that moment.

"Most certainly," Raghnall said. "Sea creatures of all kinds are afraid of them, and if any of us went overboard, they could scoop us up," he said, trying to make a scooping motion without letting go an oar, "and drop us back into the boat."

"What makes you think she would have helped us anyway?" Harry asked.

"We could have asked," Ludlow said.

"Mermaids can't be trusted," she said.

"I thought that was fairies," Raghnall answered.

"What about fair...?" Ludlow was asking when the mermaid reappeared, clinging to the blade of an oar as Raghnall pulled them up for another stroke. "Hey!" Ludlow called as Raghnall plunged the oars back into the water, but with the next stroke she was still there, giggling as she went back under.

"This is fun," she said, reappearing and disappearing again.

"Raghnall, bring her back up," Ludlow said.

"Who?" he answered.

"The mermaid," Ludlow said, but when he looked back she had let go of the oar and was bobbing beside the boat.

"Where are you going?" she asked.

"England," Ludlow answered. She seemed quite young, possibly only a year or two older than Ludlow. She had an olive complexion, long dark hair that began to curl whenever she stayed a few moments above water and eyes that shimmered turquoise as a tropical sea, even in the faint light of the moon and Harry's glow.

"Where is England?" she asked.

"North of here, we think," Ludlow answered.

"There's no land north of here for quite a distance," she said. "Isn't this boat too small for such a journey?"

"Must I remind you that she tried to kill me?" Harry asked, surprising him. She had grabbed onto Ludlow's collar and nestled in the crook of his neck, but somehow he'd forgotten that she was even there. "Enough with the small talk," she said.

"It's just that the sea can get quite rough," the mermaid continued.

"And you," Harry pointed at Raghnall, "back to rowing, please. Far away from here and quick as you can."

"We should have left you on that ship," he grumbled, and started rowing again.

Jealousy, for your information, is not a trait common to all fairies, although it often goes hand in hand with selfishness. It probably wasn't even a trait common to Harry until approximately five minutes earlier.

"I'm Isla," the mermaid said, following beside them in a back stroke.

"I'm Ludlow Osgoode," he answered, not sure why he

had told her his last name, and after a sharp pinch of his ear from Harry, he introduced the others, "and this is Harry, and he's Raghnall."

"Is she a fairy?" Isla asked, nodding her head towards his shoulder.

"I'm right here. I can hear you," Harry said. "I can even speak. I'm doing it right now."

"Can you? How grand," Isla replied. "I'd always thought fairies weren't very clever."

Raghnall laughed and then pretended to clear his throat.

"I've never met one before," she added. "I'm very pleased to make your acquaintance," she said with a smile. "And you?" Isla turned to Raghnall. "Are you a troll? Or a goblin, perhaps?"

"A goblin, ma'am," he answered, and nodded to her politely.

"Then are *you* a troll?" she asked Ludlow. He let out a laugh before the thought occurred to him that she might be insulting him.

"He's a human, genius," Harry said.

Isla stopped dead in the water and let their boat

overtake her. Ludlow looked back and then grabbed onto the oars to stop Raghnall from rowing away, but when he looked for her again, she was gone.

"If I'd known that's all I had to say to make her go away, I'd have said it the moment we met her," Harry said.

"What do we have to say to make you go away?" Raghnall asked.

"Where's she gone? I don't understand," Ludlow said.

"What's not to understand? She's afraid of humans," Harry said. "She should be afraid of fairies. Not very clever? Ha!"

Creatures human beings don't believe in are often afraid of humans and hide from them, which is why humans don't believe they exist. Mermaids are especially afraid of humans. Since most of the sightings of mermaids had been linked with the sinking of ships, sailors and fishermen had hunted mermaids for years. Little did those seamen know, mermaids were only at the scenes of those events to help them.

"So why aren't *you* afraid of humans?" Ludlow asked, turning his head slightly towards Harry.

"Because I can enchant them to see me as a huge,

hulking human male, and instead, they fear me," she answered.

"But you're not afraid of *me*," Ludlow said.

"No, of course not."

"Why not? I know you're not really a huge, hulking man," he said.

"Well, because you're small for a human, and you're kind, and you've sort of become my friend," she mumbled.

"Your friend?" he asked.

"I suppose so, yes," she answered. "Not to mention, I'm your kidnapper."

"And you, Raghnall, are you my friend?" Ludlow asked.

"Yes, I imagine I am," Raghnall said. "I've never had a friend before, or if I did I don't recall it."

"Well, you have one now," Ludlow said.

"One what?" Raghnall asked.

CHAPTER 23

One of the things that human beings and creatures human beings don't believe in have in common is that they are all afraid of the dark. Of course, each individual human being and creature has its own level of tolerance or fear, but each one is at least a little bit afraid. Ludlow, Raghnall and Harry were no different. The moon, and, indeed, most of the night sky, had been obscured by clouds for almost an hour. Except for a few scattered stars, they were surrounded by pitch blackness—no light on the horizon from a passing ship or lighthouse, or any sign of life.

Even Harry, whose light was visible to others for some distance, wasn't able to illuminate the darkness surrounding them. Her glow had been enough only to light the compass and the small patch of checkered blanket she sat on for all that time.

She pulled a corner of the blanket around herself and nestled into Ludlow's lap with a shiver. Although fairies project light, they do not project warmth. The night was growing colder, as it does, and although he hadn't been pulled into the sea, the damp had seeped into Ludlow's clothes too. The blanket from the supplies crate hardly warmed him at all, but still what he found most unbearable was that it was just...

"So dark," he said.

"Who said that?" Raghnall asked, startled.

Harry sighed and flew up to illuminate Ludlow's face.

"Oh," Raghnall said. "I'm sorry, sir. I forgot you were

there for a minute."

"It's okay, Raghnall," Ludlow said.

"It's freezing too. I don't know which is worse," Harry said, "the dark or the cold."

"I've never been in such dark or been so cold," Ludlow said. "Do you think this is what it's like to be dead?"

"That's a bit morbid, don't you think?" Harry said. "How about we save death talk for during the day, when we're home safe and sound, preferably sitting by a fire and drinking a warm beverage?"

"Why?" Ludlow asked. "Am I scaring my kidnapper?"

"No," she answered. "You're scaring Raghnall."

"No, he's not," Raghnall said. He was quiet for a moment. "Well, perhaps just a bit."

"Sorry," Ludlow said. "It's too bad we weren't on the Pacific Ocean. There are jellyfish in the Pacific that give off light."

"What's the Pacific Ocean?" Harry asked.

"Don't know everything then, do you?" Ludlow replied.

"I know how to do this," Harry said. Ludlow looked down at her, mostly covered by the blanket once more, with her fingers pressed against her temples. He couldn't figure out what she was doing, until the sea around him lit up with jellyfish. A bloom of twinkling jellies surrounded their lifeboat, bobbing just beneath the surface of the water and flashing shades of red, pink, blue, and purple. Their bells were round with lines radiating out from the centre, like the spokes of a wheel or the points of a compass. The jellies seemed to dance around them, following the lifeboat as they rowed.

"That's brilliant," Ludlow said, tears filling his eyes. He wiped them away with his sleeve, desperate not to miss anything. Carefully, so as not to tip it, he peered over the side of the boat at the swarm of jellies that stretched into the depths of the water, illuminating a school of silvery mackerel, sea anemones and corals as they passed. The sea beneath them was lit up like a sky full of fireworks.

Sometimes, in spite of everything, life can be spectacularly beautiful.

"Look at them," Ludlow said. "They're brilliant. Isn't it wonderful, Raghnall?"

"I'm afraid I can't see anything, sir," Raghnall said.

"Why not?" Ludlow asked.

As you may recall, Harry had the ability to alter human

beings' perceptions of creatures and places.

"It only works on humans," Harry said, as Raghnall continued rowing and Ludlow marvelled at the light show she had created for him in the dark water.

CHAPTER 24

A few hours later, the jellies now far behind them, Ludlow found himself immersed in darkness once more. Harry had disappeared beneath the blanket with the compass, and only the faintest glimmer of light shone through. He struggled to stay awake. After all, he hadn't slept at all that night, and the sounds of the gentle waves and the oars dragging through the water were so incredibly calming, and the dark was so incredibly tiring.

He tried closing one eye to let it rest, then opening that eye and closing the other. This strategy seemed to work, and he was quite pleased with himself, but only for a few minutes until one eye closed and the other eye followed.

Although he couldn't be certain, he might have actually been asleep when the glow of moonlight shone through his closed eyelids. His eyes popped open, but after he had spent so much time in darkness, the moon seemed brighter than the sun. He squinted and blinked to make out the shape of Raghnall in the moonlight, the hair on his head and face glistening, his head tilting backwards, mouth gaping open, eyes closed behind his glasses and his hands slowly releasing the oars.

"Raghnall!" Ludlow shouted.

He jerked awake as Ludlow launched forward and grabbed the oars before they could slip out of the round metal oarlocks and into the sea.

"What happened?" Raghnall asked.

"You fell asleep," Ludlow answered. "You let go the oars. We almost lost them."

"I'm sorry," Raghnall said.

"We'd have been set adrift!" Harry shouted, unfurling herself from the twisted blanket.

"I'm sorry," Raghnall said again, as she flew right up into his face, arms crossed. "I didn't get much sleep. It was a frightfully busy day and I only slept an hour or two on the ship before he woke me."

"I hadn't thought of that," Ludlow said. He opened his mouth to say he was sorry, but he was overtaken by another thought, and although it wasn't more important than saying he was sorry, it was important. "You remember me waking you and escaping?" Ludlow asked.

Harry uncrossed her arms and looked back at Ludlow, apparently surprised. What's more, Raghnall looked as surprised as she did.

"I do, sir," he answered. "I do."

"That's strange," Harry said.

They sat in silence until Ludlow prompted him. "Go on then. Ask what's strange."

"Why?" Raghnall asked.

Ludlow and Harry turned and stared at each other but only for a moment before she closed her eyes and shook her head. "Well," she said, "are we going to just sit here or are we going to start rowing again?"

"Right," Ludlow said. "Raghnall, teach me how to row and we'll take turns."

Rowing a boat is not the easiest of things to do when one has never done it before, even for an adult human of average size. Ludlow was not an adult human of average size. If you'll recall, he wasn't even average size for an eleven-year-old human boy.

The lesson was fairly long and tedious, with the boat jerking and moving about in every direction except forward for most of it. In time, though, Ludlow had learned to row the boat in a fairly straight line, and they were off again.

Raghnall curled up on the bottom of the boat and pulled the canvas tarp over himself to sleep.

"Good night, sir," he said.

"Good night," Ludlow answered, over Raghnall's instant snoring. Ludlow smiled and shook his head.

"That racket is going to drive me crazy," Harry said, landing on Ludlow's shoulder.

"Can't you do something to make it not sound so bad?"

"Like what?" she asked. "Cover my ears? I tried that every night on that stinking ship."

"No, I mean…"

"It literally stank," she went on.

"I mean can't you use your magic or whatever it is to make it sound like something else?" he asked. "Something more pleasant?"

"I could make it sound better to you, but I'd still be able to hear it, so no," she said.

Ludlow shook his head again.

"What will you do with him when you get back to England?" she asked.

"I hadn't thought about it, really. I suppose he could stay in the shed in our back garden. No one's gone in there for ages."

"They might when they hear that snoring or smell that smell," she said.

"I'll figure...something out," he panted, as he pulled the oars through the water.

"You must be looking forward to getting home."

"Yes. You must...be too," he answered.

"I suppose you and I will go our separate ways when we get back to England, won't we?" she asked.

"I guess so." He stopped rowing for a minute to catch his breath but quickly started again.

"Are you tired?"

"A little," he answered, wheezing. "But we have to keep going. Can you...stop me...from feeling tired?"

It seemed to Ludlow as if quite a bit of time had passed before she finally answered, "No." His arms grew numb. He felt like he had been rowing forever. Raghnall's snoring quickened and then slowed again, almost to a halt. Ludlow was wide awake and then half asleep. The moon was full and the sky clear, and then, moments later, it was cast in a net of clouds once more. An oar almost slipped from his grip. He tightened it. It slipped again, as did the other, this time into the water and Ludlow into a deep, dreamless sleep.

CHAPTER 25

It was the pain of the boat's edge pressed against his squashed face that finally woke Ludlow and not until dawn of the next morning. His eyelids were so heavy he couldn't open them, but he was awake and listening to Raghnall snore, and feeling the soreness of his cheek when he remembered where he was, who he was with and what he'd been doing: rowing.

"Ludlow!" Harry shouted. "Ludlow, the oars! You let go the oars!"

She stood on the edge of the boat and pried his left eye open with her tiny hands. The snoring stopped, the boat jerked and Ludlow saw Raghnall throw himself half overboard looking for the wayward oars. Ludlow sat straight up, and then he too was bent over the side, flailing his arms through the thick morning fog as if he was trying to push it out of the way, but the oars were nowhere in sight, even when he managed to will his other eye open.

"What have I done?" Ludlow asked.

"You've set us adrift!" Harry shouted into his ear. "We're going nowhere."

He didn't respond.

"Did you hear me?" she asked, appearing in front of his eyes just as they erupted in tears.

Creatures human beings don't believe in are often unsettled by human emotions; not because they don't have emotions themselves, but rather because they tend to believe that human beings don't have any.

"I'm sorry," Harry said in a panic. "Look, I didn't mean it!" she shouted over his sobs.

"Didn't mean it?" he cried. "But it's true. We *are* set adrift."

"I didn't mean to yell at you is what I meant. Of course, we're set adrift. We're basically doomed, but don't cry about it," she said, only causing him to cry harder and sob louder.

"That's brilliant. Well done," Raghnall said to her.

Ludlow buried his face in his hands and cried. He cried as though he'd had his heart broken and lost his best friend all at once. He cried and cried and then cried some more.

"She'll be following us by now," he eventually heard Raghnall whisper.

"Without a doubt," Harry replied, quietly. "If she's not coming after him, she'll be coming after me." Ludlow felt a pinch as Harry kneeled on his hunched back, and then felt both of her hands patting him clumsily on the shoulder. He opened and wiped his eyes and looked down at the compass lying open at his feet.

"We have to do something," Raghnall said.

"What can we do now except wait for her to catch us?" Harry asked and the compass needle slowly drifted right.

"Have you lost your mind?" Raghnall asked. "We'll never escape her a second time."

"You don't know what I'm capable of," she said.

"I think I do know what you're capable of," he grumbled.

"We might die out here," Harry said.

"We might die if she catches us. Now make yourself useful and take a quick fly round and look for those oars."

"They'll have sunk," she said.

"They float, actually," Raghnall answered.

"And what exactly do you expect me to do if I find one?

I can't even lift an oar," she said, as Ludlow finally looked up at them.

"Just get out of here," Raghnall said, shooing her away, and with a pout she turned and flew off.

Ludlow watched her fade into a dull glow before vanishing completely into the morning fog and then looked back at Raghnall, who was bent over the wooden plank he'd been sitting on, trying to pry it away from the boat's frame. He pulled and grunted and wheezed and pulled some more, until he made a sound not unlike an elephant blowing water out of its trunk, stepped back and gave the plank a good kick.

"I'm sorry, Raghnall," Ludlow said.

"It's not your fault, sir," Raghnall answered, turning and shuffling over to him.

"It is," Ludlow answered.

"It could have happened to anyone," he said, patting Ludlow on the shoulder. "It almost happened to me."

"Your memory really has improved, hasn't it?" Ludlow said with a sniffle.

"It has," Raghnall said, turning back to the plank and trying once again to pull it loose.

"What are you doing?"

"Trying to get this thwart up. I reckon I could use it to row a bit. I'd just have to row a couple of strokes on each side to keep her running true."

"True?" Ludlow asked.

"Yes, I mean straight, sir," he said. "On course."

"Oh," Ludlow answered. "Wouldn't that be awfully hard to do?"

"Well, we've got to do something. Morag'll be coming after us. No doubt she's almost on top of us already."

Someone *was* almost on top of them. Two someones, in fact. As it turned out, one had been following them closely for some time, even though they thought they'd left her far behind them.

From a young age, mermaids are taught to stay clear of and even fear humans for the reasons previously explained. Though human beings are the only creatures on or in the sea of whom mermaids are afraid, their fear is intense and instinctive. A mermaid who would go against this instinct must either be incredibly brave or simply unable to turn her back on a creature in need of help. Isla may have been both of those things.

Ludlow and Raghnall heard her voice through the fog, but neither recognized it at first.

"Who's that?" Raghnall whispered.

Ludlow shook his head.

"I think she said your name," Raghnall said, his head tilted towards the sound of her voice.

The next sound that came was the dull hum of a boat's motor. Then they clearly heard her say, "He's a human boy, truly."

"The mermaid?" Ludlow whispered.

"No," Harry said, alighting on his shoulder. "It's a boat."

"But it's not Morag?" he asked.

"No," she answered. "A fishing boat."

"Are you sure?" Ludlow asked.

"Help us!" Raghnall shouted into the mist.

"Good God," they heard the fisherman say. "It's true."

Though the engine immediately stopped, the waves that lapped against the side of the lifeboat continued to grow higher and stronger, splashing right into it when the bow of the fishing boat pierced through the fog and struck them sideways.

"I told you it was a boat!" Harry shouted over the *bang*,

crack and *sploshes*.

The impact would have tipped them all into the sea if Isla hadn't been on the other side to push the lifeboat back upright.

"Ugh," Harry said. "It *is* the mermaid."

Ludlow smiled when he saw her.

"Hi," she said with a giggle.

"Hi," he answered.

"Hi," Harry said, inserting herself between them.

"Hello down there," the fisherman called to them. He jumped at the sight of Raghnall and stepped back slightly to rub his eyes and shake his head. "It can't be." He looked down at them again and reached under his hat to scratch his head. After a few more shakes of his head and another "It can't be," he finally shouted down to Ludlow. "Boy! Rather, the least hairy boy. What's your name?"

"Harry, he can see me," Raghnall said. "You didn't enchant him."

"Sorry," she said with a shrug.

"He'd already seen Isla anyway, Raghnall," Ludlow pointed out.

"Hello?" the fisherman called again.

"My name's Ludlow," he answered. "Ludlow Osgoode."

"Well, Ludlow, I'm Michael. Michael Storey," he said. "I can take you home."

Michael Storey had a kind face. It was the worn, dark, unshaven face of an old fisherman but a kind old fisherman. His scraggly white beard and bushy eyebrows glistened with mist under the brim of a bright yellow fishing hat.

"He looks a good enough sort," Raghnall said.

"I told him all about you, Ludlow Osgoode," Isla said. "I told him you needed help to get back to England. Did I get it right?"

"Yes, England," Ludlow said. "That's right, but I thought you were afraid of humans."

"Oh, I am," she nodded vigorously, "but you needed help."

"We don't need your help," Harry said.

"How did your oar search go then?" Raghnall asked.

"I've got a rope ladder I can drop down to you!" Michael Storey shouted from above them before disappearing from view.

"We definitely need *his* help," Raghnall said, and Ludlow nodded in agreement. When Ludlow looked back up to where Michael Storey had been standing, help arrived in the form of a rather sturdy, heavy rope ladder landing squarely on his chest and knocking him backwards into the bottom of the lifeboat.

"Sorry," they heard Michael Storey say.

Raghnall picked Ludlow up and heaved him over his shoulder and began the climb up to the deck of the fishing boat.

Harry flitted up alongside, filling their ears with chatter about not needing Isla's help and how this was probably a trap and didn't they know mermaids can't be trusted, but Raghnall just swatted her away with his free hand as he would a fly.

"Is he alright?" Storey asked, as Raghnall set Ludlow down on the deck.

He still felt a bit stunned and he stumbled slightly when Raghnall let go of him, but eventually he found his footing, and the three stood looking at one another for a moment before anyone spoke.

"That's quite a powerful smell," Michael Storey said with a cough. He shook his head, and turned to Ludlow. "So, you're a boy," he said, "as in, human."

"Yes, sir," Ludlow nodded.

"And you?" He turned to Raghnall. "You are what exactly?"

"A goblin, sir," he answered, as if it was obvious.

"Right. Yes, of course, okay, and that really is a mermaid down there circling my fishing boat and the small creature with the wings, wherever she's got to, she's a fairy," he said, looking around for Harry.

"That's right, sir," Ludlow answered.

"Have I been drinking?"

"I don't know, sir," Ludlow answered.

"Please, don't call me 'sir,'" he said. "Just call me Storey. Everyone calls me Storey."

They were startled by the panicked bark of a dog as Harry emerged from the boat's wheelhouse, dishevelled and flapping wildly, with a black Labrador retriever following close behind her. Harry crashed into Ludlow's chest as Michael Storey said, "I see you've met Duchess," and grabbed the dog's collar before she pounced.

"I had a dog once," Raghnall said.

"What?" Harry asked, hanging from Ludlow's collar.

"I had a dog once," he said again. "It sounds ridiculous,

I know, but I remember it," he said, looking at Ludlow.

"A goblin with a dog?" Ludlow asked, not even realizing just how bizarre a concept it was. Dogs, you see, are highly sensitive to the existence of creatures human beings don't believe in. Such creatures know full well that a dog will alert humans to their presence and that they must, therefore, avoid dogs at all costs. Many find avoiding dogs difficult, though, because dogs are just so terribly cute.

"I'm sure of it. Her name was Belle," Raghnall continued. "I used to take her for walks on the beach."

"Walks on the beach?" Ludlow asked, looking down at Harry, who was speechless in spite of her gaping mouth.

"Well, okay," Storey said, still trying to restrain the dog. "Let's say I haven't been drinking or hit my head or fallen into a coma, and this is all actually happening. How the devil did you get out here?"

CHAPTER 26

Harry, Ludlow and Raghnall recounted their entire tale to Storey like old friends. It took them so long that the fog had time to clear, the clouds time to part and the sun time to climb half way into the sky above them before they were through. They didn't leave out a single detail—from Harry's confession: "I suppose it all started when I kidnapped him from that rather depressing party at his house"; to Ludlow's recounting: "and the banshee wanted to keep me there forever"; to Raghnall's piping in: "or at least until she finally succeeded in killing you"; then back to Harry: "And at nightfall we made our escape"; and finally over to Ludlow once more: "And we ended up here on your fishing boat."

"That's right," Raghnall said with a nod.

Storey stared at them for a moment before standing up again and lacing his fingers together behind his back. At a certain point during the retelling of their tale he'd had to sit down on a crate; it was about the moment when he learned that banshees really exist and could likely kill him, whether they wanted to or not.

"So, this is real? What you're telling me is really...real?" he asked.

"Yes, sir," they all answered.

"And, if I understood you correctly, this banshee woman is probably in hot pursuit of you and could very likely kill me?" he asked.

"Yes, sir," they all answered.

"Whether she wants to or not," Raghnall added.

You're probably afraid, as Ludlow was, that Storey decided not to help them. It would have been safer for him not to, but after much pacing and a bit of mumbling to himself he finally said, "Right. Well, grab the rest of your things out of that dinghy and we'd better shove off before she gets wind of us."

Relieved, Ludlow rushed back to the ladder, but Raghnall was already there.

"I'll get our things, sir," Raghnall said, starting the climb back down to the lifeboat. "You stay here," he called.

"Oh, no," Storey said to Ludlow. "I'm sorry, no," he lowered his voice. "You can come, but the others..."

Ludlow's eyes widened. "I can't just *leave* them," he said.

"But they're not, you know...human, are they?"

Harry alighted on Ludlow's shoulder, hands on hips. "What's so great about humans anyway?" she asked.

"Ignore her," Ludlow said to Storey. "Look, I wouldn't have escaped without them."

Storey's face twisted into about a hundred different expressions. He looked from Ludlow to Harry and back to Ludlow. He removed his hat to scratch his head twice and opened his mouth as if to speak four times, only to let out sighs in the end.

"They'll die out here," Ludlow finally said, looking down at Raghnall, who had stopped halfway down the ladder, not moving another single rung. Isla clung to the side of the lifeboat, watching and waiting.

Storey peered over the railing at Raghnall and Isla himself and let out another long sigh. "Alright then, they can come. Just hurry," he said. "We've probably been hanging around here too long already."

"Hurry, Raghnall!" Ludlow shouted down to him.

Raghnall dropped into the lifeboat and scurried around it, collecting supplies and cramming them into the already overflowing burlap sack, while Isla circled and watched, asking him questions about goblins and fairies and whatever in the world a banshee was, because it sounded absolutely horrible.

"I've heard quite enough about this banshee, thank you!" Storey shouted to her as he paced along the railing of the fishing boat, looking down at the lifeboat and then up to the horizon. "Oh, wait," he said, squinting and pointing. "Is there something there?" he asked.

Ludlow looked up at a glint of bright light in the distance, until it was totally obscured by the burlap sack, hurtling through the air towards them and stopping only when it struck Storey's face.

He was suddenly flat on his back, hands cupped around his nose, shouting a muffled "Good God!" and then, removing his hands from his face as if to check for blood, "What've you got in that thing?" Storey asked.

"Just some books, paintings, a hand drill and an alarm clock," Ludlow said.

"Oh, is that all?" Storey asked, pulling himself to his feet. "What the devil do you need those for?"

"And a mostly empty water bottle, half a loaf of bread, a box of chocolates and some life vests," Raghnall said, as he climbed back onto the deck.

"Life vests," Storey said. "Yes, that must be what nearly broke my nose. Just a thought, next time you're going to toss a bag of heavy objects into the boat, how about shouting something like, 'Look out,' okay?"

Raghnall nodded.

"Well," Storey said, "welcome aboard the *Lyonesse*. Make yourselves at home."

"Thank you," they all said, as they scattered about to explore it.

The *Lyonesse* was less than half the size of the *Anathema*. It had a small main deck, a glassed-in wheelhouse and a cabin below deck with enough room to comfortably accommodate two small human beings at a time or one large one. It had two sleeping berths and a makeshift kitchen with a table and chair, still laden with the pot of tea and plate of toasted crumpets and strawberry-rhubarb jam that Storey hadn't had a chance to finish that morning.

"There's fresh water in the cabin," Storey called, as Ludlow reached the table, "and deodorant spray. Help yourselves," he said. "Take as much as you like." Ludlow only barely heard him over the sound of his own mouth crunching down on a stone-cold crumpet.

What was loud enough to hear were the sounds of the anchor dropping, and the resounding *crack* that followed. Ludlow moved towards a porthole and looked out just in time to watch the lifeboat slowly fill with water and sink into the sea.

"Why have you done that?" he heard Raghnall ask.

"Well, this Morose woman will be looking for you on a lifeboat, not on a fishing boat," Storey said. "This way, we'll avoid her coming across the empty dinghy and suspecting you've switched vessels."

"Morag," Raghnall corrected him.

"Pardon?"

"Her name's not Morose, it's Morag."

"Some might have congratulated me on my clever idea, but correcting me is another way to go, I suppose," Storey said before his voice was drowned out by the raising anchor.

Ludlow stopped to gulp down the last of the lukewarm tea from Storey's teacup as he walked back past the kitchen table. Still licking the jam from his fingers, he re-emerged above deck and followed Storey into the wheelhouse. He wandered around it, running his sticky fingers over the various buttons, knobs, gauges and instruments and reading what everything was aloud to himself.

He climbed onto a stool beside Storey and watched him plot out their location on a map, putting them somewhere west of the Isles of Scilly in the Celtic Sea.

"Is that where we are?" Ludlow asked, pointing a finger and leaving behind a streaky, pink smudge.

"Should be," Storey answered. "I see you ate my breakfast."

"I'm sorry," Ludlow said. "I was just so hungry."

"It's alright, Lud."

"I was going the wrong way," Ludlow said.

"You're only a boy," Storey said, patting the top of Ludlow's head. "Don't fret. You've done quite well to get through what you've gone through so far. What are you, about ten years old?" he asked.

"Just turned eleven," he answered.

Storey continued talking, but Ludlow had stopped listening. He was lost in a memory of his birthday. "I didn't get any presents this year," he had suddenly remembered.

"Sorry?" Storey asked.

"For my birthday," Ludlow explained. "I don't think there was a cake either. I don't remember blowing out any candles."

"Well, that's a shame," Storey answered. "Your fairy friend did say it was a rather depressing party. Still, as I was saying, you must be looking forward to getting home, you know, even in spite of the 'no cake' issue."

"Right," Ludlow said.

A rather awkward silence followed until...

"Erm, where have your friends got to, eh?" Storey asked.

CHAPTER 27

When Ludlow found them, Raghnall was safely nestled next to Duchess in a pile of ropes on the deck, leafing through the worn pages of his copy of *Peter Pan*, and Harry fluttered and hovered above him watching the horizon.

"What are you doing flitting about up there?" Raghnall asked.

"Keeping an eye out for Morag," she answered. Her glow splashed across the deck and pages of the book like a beam of light reflecting off of glass.

"She won't be looking for us on a fishing boat, will she?" Raghnall said. "She'll be looking for the lifeboat. Now set yourself down somewhere," he grumbled. "You're giving me a headache."

Ludlow leaned over the railing beside them and looked

down into the water for Isla. She seemed to have slipped back into the sea while they were exploring the fishing boat.

"Ludlow, sir, would you tell her I'm right?" Raghnall asked.

Ludlow lifted his gaze to the horizon. The air had grown quite warm, even hazy in the sun, and although he could make out the shapes of some ships and vessels on the horizon, he couldn't tell if any of them were the *Anathema*.

Raghnall has a point, though, he thought. Even if one of the ships was the *Anathema*, Morag wouldn't know to look for them on a fishing boat.

"He is right," Ludlow said, sitting down next to Raghnall and Duchess. Over Raghnall's shoulder he noticed an old library return card slot on the inside cover of *Peter Pan*. Just as the gold book plate in his copy of *Alice's Adventures in Wonderland* had read "A Gift to Penzance Library," the card slot had a stamp on it, also from Penzance Library.

"Is that a library book, Raghnall?" Ludlow asked.

"I don't know," he answered.

"What's a library book?" Harry asked.

"Well," Ludlow said, "a library is a place where you can

go to borrow a book..."

"Borrow?" Harry said, finally landing on the deck in front of them.

"Yes," Ludlow said.

"Doesn't that mean you have to bring it back?" she asked.

"Exactly," Ludlow said. "Usually within a few weeks' time."

"Well, that's terrible," Raghnall said. "I've had these books much longer than a few weeks."

"How did you get them?" Ludlow asked.

"I don't recall," he answered. "I've had them for as long as I can remember."

"So he's stolen them?" Harry asked.

"Oh dear, does that make me a criminal?" Raghnall asked, clutching the book to his chest. Ludlow hadn't seen him so upset before.

"A criminal," Harry said, shaking her head.

"I don't think it's actually a crime, Raghnall," Ludlow said. He wondered if he should tell them that although not returning a library book on time might not actually be a crime, stealing all of the other things he had stolen and kidnapping a child definitely were, but he didn't have to. Raghnall had already figured it out.

"We stole you too, didn't we?" he asked, looking down at the empty card slot.

"Yes," Ludlow said.

"That's different," Harry said.

"How?" Raghnall asked.

"Well, we're bringing him back," she answered.

"Then I should bring back these library books," Raghnall said.

"You could return them, of course," Ludlow said.

"Then that's what I'll do," he said with a proud smile. "Do you think they'd let me borrow some more?" he asked.

Ludlow suddenly started imagining himself walking into a library with a goblin to return overdue library books and people screaming and running through the aisles with their eyes bulging out of their heads and their arms flailing in the air. The police would no doubt arrive, although they probably wouldn't care too much about the overdue books. Ludlow realized then and there that he could never bring Raghnall to a library, except possibly on Halloween, but he couldn't bear to tell him.

"I'm sure they would," Ludlow said.

"Are you being serious?" Harry asked. "He's a goblin."

"Oh," Raghnall said, removing his glasses. "She's right."

"If I'm not around, you'll have to hide him," she said, "from everyone."

"Hide?" Raghnall asked. "From *everyone*?"

"Look at you," Harry said. "You could never pass for a human."

Raghnall looked at Ludlow with pleading eyes, blue as the sea and sky around them.

"Raghnall," Ludlow said, "didn't your eyes used to be brown?"

It was an intriguing question. Sadly, there was no time for an answer.

CHAPTER 28

A wail. A great, resounding wail churned up the sea around them and tossed them all from their rope bed and across the deck.

"What's happening? Is it her?" Storey asked, as Raghnall and Ludlow tripped over Duchess through the open door of the wheelhouse.

"It's Morag," Harry answered, as she darted in above them. "She's found us."

"But how?" Ludlow asked.

"That doesn't matter now!" Storey shouted, spinning the wheel in his hands to steady the *Lyonesse*. At that moment, a huge wave curled over the bow of the fishing boat, hurling a long, gnarled bough of driftwood right across the window. It landed with a *crack* and a *bang*, sending them jumping back, and then another ear-piercing wail emerged from behind them, pushing them all forward again.

"I can't have this," Storey said. He handed the wheel over to Raghnall. "Hold her steady," he said. "I've got to get that thing clear of the window."

He stumbled out onto the slippery deck and skidded uncontrollably to the edge, until the railing stopped him from sliding into the sea. A final bone-chilling wail filled their ears, shaking them all from their insides out, before the sea curiously calmed. The waves subsided, the boat settled and steadied, and all was quiet. So quiet that the one sound that finally arose was so loud, it was almost deafening. It was a sound unlike any they had ever heard and almost impossible to describe. Imagine the sound of a thousand fingernails scraping against a blackboard, and a thousand forks scraping against eight thousand teeth, a car crash and a shelf of musical instruments being knocked to the ground, and you will come close to imagining the sound of a sea monster about to strike.

It spewed up out of the water high into the sky above them, an enormous, never-ending snake-like creature with the head of a catfish. Fishermen are almost always disappointed to reel in a catfish, so you can understand that being attacked by one must be even more of a disappointment.

"Wonderful," Storey grumbled. "A giant catfish."

Duchess bolted onto the deck and up to the railing, barking hysterically at the creature and then, as if she had realized that this was quite possibly the most foolish thing she had ever done, abruptly turned and ran cowering back into the wheelhouse and continued to bark at it through the window.

"Thank you, Duchess!" Storey shouted, grabbing the long branch from the window with both hands. "That was unhelpful."

It hadn't been entirely unhelpful, though. She hadn't succeeded in scaring the sea monster away; however, it did seem confused, and as Storey edged towards it, waving the large stick and shouting for it to get back, it seemed even more confused. For some time it hovered there, watching him thrust the branch towards it, observing.

"Can't you do something, Harry?" Ludlow asked.

The sea monster began to sway back and forth.

"Like what?" she asked.

The sea monster seemed to recoil before moving in closer once more.

"It's going to kill him!" Ludlow shouted. "Please, do something."

The sea monster pulled back again and then lunged at Storey. It plucked him from the deck with its fishy lips and made a sour face before spitting him out again.

"Harry, *please!*" Ludlow shouted.

It looked as if it were about to repeat the routine when suddenly the sea monster turned into an enormous adorable white seal pup.

"Awwww," Storey said with a tilt of his head.

"What's happening?" Ludlow asked, and then noticed that Harry was perched on the wheel with her eyes closed and her fingers pressed against both temples. "Are you doing that?" he asked her.

"Stop talking," she snapped. "I'm trying to concentrate."

"But that means it's still a sea monster, only he doesn't know it's a sea monster," Raghnall said.

It was true. The sea monster was still a sea monster—giant, slobbering and no doubt hungry for another mouthful of salty fisherman—but to the humans on board, it had been transformed into possibly the cutest thing they had ever laid eyes on. Storey got to his feet again, dropped the branch onto the deck and ran up to hug it, like a long-lost friend.

"Look at this!" he shouted back to them. "Isn't it adorable?" he asked, as he clung to its fur and let it lift him into the air.

"What's the plan here, Harry?" Raghnall asked. "How's this supposed to work?"

The sea monster dipped and swayed, apparently trying to shake off his attacker, but Storey wouldn't let go.

"You're the cutey-utest baby seal pup in the whole wide world," he said, burying his face in the fur that wasn't really there.

"This is the strangest thing I've ever seen," Raghnall

said, shaking his head.

The sea monster shook its head too, wildly, until Storey couldn't keep hold of its slimy scales anymore and slipped back onto the deck of the fishing boat with a thud. Ludlow ran out onto the deck to pull him back, but he didn't need to. Storey was obviously seeing the sea monster for what it really was once more, and was quickly on his feet and hurrying himself and Ludlow back towards the wheelhouse. "What the devil came over me?" he shouted.

Ludlow stumbled and fell. He tried to push himself up, but his hands slipped out from under him. He looked up to see the horror on Storey's face, then turned his head to look down the sea monster's throat, and there wasn't much to see after that. It's quite dark inside a sea monster.

If you're reading this book, you've probably never had the bad fortune to be swallowed whole by a sea monster. If you have been swallowed whole by a sea monster and survived, you are an impressive child, indeed. Escaping the bowels of a sea monster is no easy feat.

After sloshing around inside the creature's mouth, struggling to breathe and mostly swallowing seawater, Ludlow found himself sliding down the creature's tongue and into what he could only assume was its belly. The air was thin and his ears kept popping, and he realized that the sea monster was returning to the bottom of the sea with Ludlow inside of it.

It was completely dark; the mucous in the monster's stomach stung his skin. With one hand, Ludlow felt his pockets for something, anything, to use to irritate the monster's stomach and send it back to the surface. With the other hand, he used his fingernails to scrape every part of the monster's insides he could reach, until he felt the tube of matches and compass in his pocket, and had an idea. He unscrewed the cylinder and carefully lifted the cap just enough to allow one match to spill out. He was being tossed around inside the stomach of a sea monster, after all, and couldn't allow the matches to fall about the place. He grabbed the compass and felt for the rough, engraved side and struck the match against it. There was just enough air left for the match to light. Ludlow waved it about and saw where he was for the first time.

He looked for where he had fallen from and saw what he thought was the creatures' tongue at the end of a long, slimy tunnel. The match was burning down. With his free hand he grabbed onto the flesh of the monster's throat, just as the match fizzled out singeing his fingertips. The smell of sulfur filled the air, and a thin wisp of smoke followed him through the tunnel. He felt his ears pop again and again as he pulled himself along, and realized the monster was climbing to the surface. As he reached the monster's mouth it opened wide, and a churning, gurgling sound arose from beneath Ludlow's feet before he was disgustingly coughed out. He was free of the sea monster but not the sea.

He plunged into the salty water, right in the midst of a school of anchovies, most of whom had probably just had the fright of their lives when a rather agitated sea monster came streaking past them. They scattered instantly, leaving Ludlow alone in that plot of sea, rushing to the surface. He choked on the seawater in his throat, but was soon breathing fresh air. Before he could even open his eyes or cry out for help, he heard the hum of a motor and the voices of his friends calling out to him.

"Grab the ladder, sir!" Raghnall shouted as it splashed into the water in front of Ludlow. As he climbed, he heard the heart-stopping sound of the sea monster behind him preparing to strike again.

Raghnall grabbed Ludlow by the hand and pulled him into the boat as it jerked and sharply turned. Ludlow wiped his eyes and looked up to see the sea monster recoiling again, but this time, instead of striking, it kept recoiling, edging back farther and farther from the fishing boat, watching something under the surface.

"What's it doing?" Ludlow asked.

"It's leaving," Raghnall said.

"See?" Harry said. "My plan worked."

"Your plan," Raghnall said. "A seal pup? That was a plan?" He shook his head.

"*You* saw it?" Harry asked.

"Who cares, eh?" Storey called from the wheelhouse. "Let's just get as far away from it as possible."

Ludlow watched it turn and dive back into the sea, its long body arcing over the water as it plunged back down into the depths and its whale-like tail slapping the surface before it disappeared from sight. As the water calmed again, Ludlow noticed the flick of a smaller tail that seemed to wave at him before it too disappeared into the deep.

Sea creatures of all kinds, if you'll recall, are afraid of mermaids.

CHAPTER 29

Ludlow stood alone in the cabin below deck, listening to the muffled voices of his friends up above as he pulled one of Storey's t-shirts, which was about eight sizes too large for him, over his head. He looked down at the trousers Storey had cut off below the knees for him and the too-long socks on his feet, realizing he looked ridiculous, but was relieved to be warm and dry. His wet clothes had been washed and wrung out and were now draped over a rope Storey had stretched across the cabin, almost touching the ceiling. Ludlow climbed into one of the two bunks. He pulled the blankets up over his head and turned to bury his face in a pillow as you do when you're upset, trying to hide from your problems and hoping they'll just go away. When the air got too heavy he pushed the blankets back and, sadly, but obviously, his problems hadn't gone anywhere.

The fishing boat struck a wave and the burlap sack spilled open onto the floor of the cabin. Ludlow didn't move. He laid in the bunk looking listlessly about the cabin. His clothes swung on the makeshift clothesline, the thin cotton curtains swung on their rods and the light fixture swung from the ceiling. His telescope rolled out of the sack, followed by two of Raghnall's books. Ludlow still didn't budge. The copy of *The Lion, the Witch and the Wardrobe* slid across the floor and fell open against the base of the other bunk. Something was written on one of the first pages in ink. As the book slammed shut, Ludlow was out of bed and on his feet. He snatched the book from the floor and flipped it open again, looking for the page with the inscription and found it just as Raghnall opened the hatch above him.

"Well," Ludlow heard Storey say, "the good thing about that scrape with the seal is it seems to have given us a bit of a push ahead of Moron, eh?"

"Morag," Harry said.

"And it was a sea monster, not a seal," Raghnall called over his shoulder as he trotted down the stairs into the cabin.

"Yes, well, the point is, I don't see any sign of her, so

let's look at the bright side. There are so few of them," Storey said. "Bright sides, that is."

"What've you got there?" Raghnall asked.

"You tell me," Ludlow answered, holding the book open in front of him for Raghnall to read the name *Ronnie* and beneath that, the words *Room 18 - Mrs. Littlemore*.

Raghnall just looked at him blankly.

"Who's Ronnie?" Ludlow asked.

"I don't know," Raghnall answered, straightening his glasses and looking at it more closely.

"This is a school book. Is Ronnie another boy you helped kidnap?" Ludlow asked. "Is he the one who escaped?"

"I don't think I ever kidnapped another boy," Raghnall answered, scratching his head.

"Then maybe Ronnie's a girl. We call my cousin Veronica 'Ronnie,'" Ludlow said.

"I don't remember ever kidnapping a girl either," Raghnall said.

"Well that doesn't mean you didn't do it," Ludlow said.

"I remember kidnapping you now, though, so if I had kidnapped someone else, I'd probably remember that too, wouldn't I?" Raghnall asked.

"Maybe," Ludlow said, finally lowering the book. "But this is definitely a school book," he said, reading it one last time before closing it. "Room 12 must be a classroom and Mrs. Littlemore must be a teacher. She must be," he said.

Raghnall didn't seem to be listening anymore. He had pulled open a drawer beneath the unused bunk and was rifling through it.

"The name sounds familiar, though," Raghnall eventually said.

"Which name?" Ludlow asked. "Ronnie?"

"Yes," he answered, as Ludlow watched him open and rummage through drawer after drawer, until he finally produced a pair of long whitish socks. "I think I knew someone named Ronnie."

"When?" Ludlow asked.

"I don't know. Maybe Ronnie is a character in a book," he said. "Ronnie sounds like a human name, doesn't it?" He sat back on the bunk and pulled the socks over his hairy feet, one by one.

"It is a human name," Ludlow answered, but as much as he wanted to figure out who Ronnie was, he couldn't ignore what Raghnall was doing anymore. "What are you doing there?"

"Putting on socks," Raghnall answered.

"Why?" he asked.

"Well, because my feet are cold. Why do you wear socks?" he asked, seeming confused by the conversation, which only confused Ludlow more.

"What's going on?" Ludlow asked. "Just when I think I've got my head wrapped around all of this, it turns out I don't. How did your memory get so much better? How could you have had a dog? How come your feet are cold and you've decided you need to put on socks for the first time since I met you? Your feet are covered in hair!"

"Well," Raghnall said, looking at his feet and scratching his chin, "when you put it that way, yes, I suppose it is all a bit strange," he said, before planting his index finger firmly in the centre of his forehead. Goblins, like humans, sometimes use their fingers in this way to help them think.

"I'm sorry. I didn't mean to shout," Ludlow said.

"That's okay, Ludlow," Raghnall answered with a warm smile and then went back to thinking.

Ludlow climbed back into his bunk and looked out the porthole, past the reflection of his dirty face and mussed up hair at the rippling water and clear blue sky. *If Storey can't see any sign of the Anathema, maybe we really have shaken her this time*, he thought for a moment, then wondered, *But how did she find us at all?*

They sat quietly in the cabin for a time, listening to the rumbling of the engine and churning wake that followed behind the fishing boat. The raspy caw of a seagull grew louder and louder, and suddenly the sound of Duchess's nails could be heard clicking back and forth across the deck above them.

"Where did you get to?" they heard Storey ask.

"You're going the wrong way, you know. We should turn back," Harry said.

"Shoo, fairy. Shoo!" Storey shouted. "Duchess, would you stop that infernal pacing and lie down?" he asked.

"How did she find us?" Raghnall asked.

"I was asking myself that same question," Ludlow said. He turned to see Raghnall lying on the opposite bunk, looking out the porthole above it, just as Ludlow was.

"She should still be looking for the lifeboat," Raghnall said. "There's no way she could know we're on a fishing boat." The glass fogged up as he spoke into it. Ludlow saw him rub the glass with his sleeve. "Hello?" he asked. "What's this?"

"What's what?" Ludlow asked, climbing onto the bunk beside him and pressing his face against the glass. Something was swimming alongside the *Lyonesse*, just close enough to the surface for them to know something was there but not close enough for them to figure out what.

"Do you see it?" Raghnall asked, pointing. "Is it another sea monster? Or Isla?"

"I don't know," Ludlow said. "Maybe we'd see it better from the deck," he said, and almost as soon as he'd finished getting the words out he had pulled his shoes back on and the two of them were halfway up the stairs. They didn't make it to the railing, though, or out onto the deck or even to the top of the staircase. Another shrill distant wail froze them stiff before they made it to the hatch.

—

CHAPTER 30

"**N**o!" Storey shouted, appearing at the top of the stairs. "Get below deck, all of you." He waved Duchess and Harry into the cabin as Ludlow watched a blanket of dense, grey clouds pull across the sky above them. "A storm is coming," he said, "a squall," as a great wave lashed against the side of the boat.

They watched Storey stumble and fall to his knees under a shower of seawater before he pushed the hatch closed.

"No," Ludlow said, trying to push it open again. "Raghnall, help me!" he called over his shoulder, but Raghnall had slinked back down the stairs into the heart of the cabin. When Ludlow turned to look at him, he saw Raghnall cowering in the centre of the room. Though he swayed and jolted from side to side as the waves struck the boat, it was still clear that he was quivering with fright. A glow behind Raghnall that followed him to and fro revealed that Harry was as afraid as he was.

"A squall," Harry said, a tremor in her voice. "She's brought on a squall now."

"It's going to kill him," Ludlow said.

"You don't think," Raghnall asked Harry over his shoulder, "it could turn into..."

"Ghost water?" Harry asked.

"Help me!" Ludlow shouted.

"I'm sorry, Ludlow," Raghnall said, his eyes closed and his head shaking.

"Harry?" Ludlow asked.

"I'm protecting him," she called from behind Raghnall.

Only Duchess stood with Ludlow on the stairs, howling at the storm and whimpering for her master, as he gave another futile push against the heavy hatch. Though he pushed with all the strength he could muster, it wasn't much, and the wind pushed back harder. It rattled the windows, creaked through the hull of the boat and whistled and screamed through the few cracks in the hatch. Ludlow gave one last push before his strength gave out, and he rested his head on his trembling arm.

"She's going to kill Storey," he said.

Just then, the hatch blew open wide. Without hesitation Ludlow took two steps up, climbing only far enough to peer out of the opening before another gust slammed the hatch back down, right onto his head.

CHAPTER 31

Ludlow awoke to find himself seated once again on the antique chair in the front hallway of his house. His clothes were damp and he shivered with cold. The hallway was still filled with dark-coloured umbrellas and rubber wellies. Toby had gone from the pile of boots where he'd once slept, but they were all still either crumpled or knocked over. No one had come by since to put them upright.

Ludlow wondered why he was sitting in the chair alone in the hallway, when clearly the house was full of people who were probably either getting dry by the fire in the lounge or warming themselves with a cup of tea in the kitchen, as any sensible person would be doing in the circumstances. Since he couldn't remember why he was sitting there in the first place, he thought maybe he didn't need to keep sitting there at all. Just as he was about to jump down from the chair, the front door swung open, and his cousin Veronica burst into the house. He only caught a glimpse of her curly red hair under the hood of her raincoat before the wind ripped the door from her hands and she spun around to grab it back. A swirl of wet leaves and wayward raindrops had poured into the hall by the time she managed to push the door shut behind her.

"Ronnie," Ludlow said. "I think I was just talking about you."

She stood facing away from Ludlow for a minute, panting and then quietly whimpering with her forehead pressed against the closed door.

"Are you alright?" he asked.

"Of course I'm not alright," she said, finally turning and pulling off her raincoat. "Everybody keeps asking if I'm alright," she said, giving it a shake and hanging it on a coat hook.

That's when Ludlow noticed all of the dark coats hung up on the wall, to accompany all of the rain boots and umbrellas.

"Why would I be alright?" she asked, and kicked off her

polka dotted wellies one by one, pulled and straightened her tights and then stood looking at him. Veronica was thirteen with a fair, freckled face that was often scowling, though it wasn't at that moment.

"Oh, Luddy," she said, her expression one of pity. "I'm sorry for snapping." She pulled a crumpled tissue from her pocket and handed it to him. "After all, you must be even more gutted than I am."

"Gutted? Why?" he asked, as a light flashed through the frosted glass door. "What's happened?"

"Don't you remember?" she asked between flashes.

"No," he answered.

"You will."

CHAPTER 32

Ludlow awoke with a crowd around him. He stared up at the ceiling of the cabin, past the concerned faces of Raghnall, Harry and Duchess, to the swaying light fixture, which flickered twice more before finally going out completely with a loud *pop*.

"We thought we'd lost you," Harry said, now beaming brightly in the darkened cabin. She disappeared from view, leaving only a glow behind her as she hugged Ludlow around the neck.

"What happened?" Ludlow asked.

"You were knocked unconscious," Raghnall said, taking off his glasses and polishing them with one of the clean socks he'd scrounged. "The hatch came down right on top of your head and sent you tumbling. You gave us the fright of our lives."

"We're hardly bothered by the storm anymore," Harry said, reappearing above him.

"We really aren't," Raghnall said. "So long as it's just a storm."

"What else would it be?" Ludlow asked, sitting up. His head suddenly throbbed. Raghnall answered, but for a moment everything sounded to Ludlow as though he were listening to it from under water. He hadn't understood another word until...

"They say it's horrible," he finally heard Harry say.

"I heard it's terrible," Raghnall said, more clearly.

"Unnatural," Harry said.

Duchess just panted.

"What is?" Ludlow asked again.

They both replied, "Ghost water."

You have surely never heard of ghost water, and rightly so. Only two human beings in the world are known to have experienced it and survived to tell the tale. The first was a young Canadian leisure fisherman from Saint John, New Brunswick, named Noel D. Adams. On his way back to shore one fall evening, he was caught in a storm on the Bay of Fundy, which turned into violent, boat-capsizing ghost water. Although he survived by the skin of his teeth, since he had such a terrible reputation for staying out until all hours of the night and lying to his mother about where he'd been, nobody believed his fantastic story, no matter how he insisted it was true. He was so maddened by the whole experience that he went back to university and obtained degrees in the fields of meteorology, anthropology and marine biology and has since become the world's most renowned expert on all mythological phenomena and creatures, that is to say, phenomena and creatures human beings don't believe in or have never heard of.

He has also sworn off lying forever.

Luckily for our friends, this storm would not turn into ghost water. It was, nevertheless, a harrowing experience. You are unlikely to hear the average fisherman use the expression, "Don't worry, it's just a storm." Even the mildest storm at sea can be dangerous to seamen, but a storm brought on by a banshee is almost as mythic in proportions as she is. The wind stronger, the rain harder, the sea wild and unrelenting. In this case, Morag had summoned a squall: a sudden, violent wind and rain storm that would dissipate just as suddenly as it had begun, but possibly not before the *Lyonesse* had sunk to the bottom of the sea.

CHAPTER 33

You may be wondering how exactly a banshee's wail can cause a death, and the answer all depends on the victim. A frail older man with a weak heart may suffer a heart attack at the sound of a banshee's wail, but a generally fit and healthy fisherman and a young boy with a strong heart are much more difficult to kill, and at sea there aren't many ways to kill a healthy human. Only a few come to mind: (1) death by dehydration and/or starvation (which probably would have happened to Ludlow already if Isla and Storey hadn't intervened), (2) death at the hands (or mouth) of a man-eating sea creature (which almost happened), and (3) death by drowning (which was still a possibility).

The waves crashed against the portholes, water actually spilling in around the edges, as Ludlow, Raghnall and Harry struggled to push open the hatch. Duchess scratched at it as the others backed away preparing to push again, until another violent wave struck the front of the boat and sent them all hurtling down the stairs.

Ludlow clambered to his feet and rushed to a porthole. He strained to see through the waves and the sea foam they left behind, but all there was to see was more waves, more driving rain, and a black sky. That is, until the flashes of light began. It wasn't lightning—that would have lit the entire sky. It wasn't the sun—the sun was completely eclipsed by storm clouds. It was only a spot of light flickering in the distance. He started to turn back towards the hatch but was suddenly gripped with suspicion that the bursts of light were a signal. He clung to the frame of the porthole to steady himself and watched the light flash short twice, long once, short again. *Morse code*, he thought. He'd read about it in the M volume of the *Encyclopaedia Britannica*, but didn't remember how to decipher the letters.

It's just as well, though, because the flashing stopped and just as it did, another piercing, unearthly wail resounded through the cabin as a wave bigger than any Ludlow had ever seen grew out of the sea and barrelled towards them.

"Hold on to something!" Ludlow shouted, looking for

something to grab onto himself as the wave struck. In an instant, they were all on the floor except Harry, listening to the roar of water rushing over the deck above them, then muffled shouting as Storey cursed the storm with words Ludlow wasn't allowed to say or ever repeat and then, nothing. At least, there were no more sounds of a storm, only the sound of water dripping from the deck back into the sea.

Just as it had before, the sea slowly settled, the waves receded, and the world outside grew quiet. Though the portholes were now coated with a film of froth and foam, the glow of daylight suddenly shone through. The three looked at one another, struggled to their feet and then slowly climbed the stairs once more with Duchess close behind. This time Ludlow was able to push the hatch open with only the tips of his fingers. Glittering streams of water trickled in onto them as he did. The storm had already passed, which Ludlow thought could only mean one thing.

"It's got him," he said, as they climbed up onto the deck.

They rushed from one end of the boat to the other, looking overboard for any sign of Storey.

"He's there!" Raghnall called from the bow, shouting to

be heard over Duchess's sudden barking beside him.

"Where?" Ludlow asked.

"On that beach," Raghnall said, pointing.

"Beach?" Harry asked, as she and Ludlow arrived at the railing alongside them.

"Yes, that...beach," Raghnall said, his eyes opening wide.

"We're going to wreck on that island, you blunderhead!" she shouted. "Do something."

"Oh, bloody hell!" he shouted. "Where did that island even come from?" he asked, stumbling into the wheelhouse. He grabbed onto the wheel. It wouldn't budge. "Hold on!" he shouted as the others filed in behind him. "Brace yourselves," he said, as the boat ran aground on the rocky beach of an island that seemed to have appeared out of nowhere.

While a great many phenomena and creatures human beings don't believe in actually do exist, spontaneously appearing islands do not, unless they have been summoned into existence by means of a spell or incantation or as the result of a wish being granted. This was a real island, which had been there for countless years before their boat was thrust onto it and would no doubt still be there for many more years to come. The problem, rather, was that the squall had sent them veering so far off course that they were no longer where they thought they were.

When the boat finally jerked to a halt, the foursome found themselves in a tangled pile on the floor.

"That island wasn't on the map," Ludlow said, as they struggled to free themselves from one another.

"We're not where we're supposed to be," Harry said, sitting upright on his chest and plucking long black dog hairs from her tunic. "She's sent us off course. We're lost," she said, as Ludlow picked her up by her hood and set her down on the floor of the wheelhouse. When he finally squirmed free of Raghnall and Duchess, he scrambled out to the railing, first on his knees and then on foot, and was only relieved for a moment to see Michael Storey sprawled out on the beach with Isla lying beside him.

"Wake up," Ludlow heard her say, as she tried to nudge Storey back to consciousness.

"Oh, no!" Ludlow shouted. "No!"

"What?" Harry asked, appearing next to him.

"He's drowned."

CHAPTER 34

Goblins are not known for being proficient in mouth-to-mouth respiration, especially with their snouts not being the ideal shape for performing the procedure even on another goblin, let alone a human. Moreover, most goblins and creatures human beings don't believe in have never even heard of mouth-to-mouth respiration. Ludlow and Harry were both understandably confused when Raghnall leapt from the deck of the ship and went tearing across the beach shouting, "Leave it to me! I've trained for this!"

When they arrived on the scene, Raghnall had already tilted Storey's head to clear the water from his airways and was pinching Storey's nose, ready to breathe into his mouth. It was an awkward first attempt, with his four short breaths seeming to go mostly sideways, blowing sand from Storey's cheeks.

"What are you doing?" Harry asked, as Ludlow kneeled beside them. She was, however, the only one who hadn't realized what he was doing. Even Isla had seen this before. Raghnall put his ear to Storey's mouth and then tried again, this time with Ludlow clasping his hands around the end of Raghnall's snout to force the air in the right direction. Raghnall listened again, but apparently heard nothing. He checked for a pulse, but didn't seem sure. He gave a third round of breaths. He listened again.

Ludlow, Harry and Isla all seemed to be holding their breath by that time, and just as Ludlow finally let out a gasp himself, Storey began choking on the water in his airways and rolled heavily onto his side.

"Thank God," Raghnall said, falling backwards onto the

beach while Storey spit seawater into the sand.

"How?" Harry asked.

"What?" Raghnall asked.

"Yes, how?" Ludlow asked, as he began patting Storey's back.

"I'm okay, Lud," Storey said, stifling a cough. "I'll be okay."

"Was that some kind of goblin black magic?" Harry asked, clearly disturbed by the event. "He was dead, and you brought him back to life. No creature can do that," Harry said. "A witch couldn't do it," she said, fluttering past him and then turning to fly past again in the other direction, as if pacing the air. "Not a warlock. Not a wizard," she went on, shaking her head. "Even those obnoxious know-it-all genies can't bring someone back from the dead. You could rub one of those lamps until you wore a hole in it, it just wouldn't happen." She was almost talking to herself now as she paced, and as she spoke, Raghnall's face changed too.

"She's right," he said, confused. "No creature can do that."

"There is one creature that can," Isla said.

"Really?" Harry asked, disbelieving.

"I've seen it done before. Never from so near, though."

"And what creature is that, Miss Clever-fins?" Harry asked and Isla, Storey and Ludlow answered in unison.

"Humans."

Under ordinary circumstances, when they hadn't just been shipwrecked on an island in the middle of nowhere, and if a rabidly mad banshee hadn't still been on their tails, they might have sat pondering how Raghnall had learned mouth-to-mouth respiration for longer than the few moments they had just spent on it. But they were shipwrecked, a crazed banshee was still hunting them, and as soon as Storey was able to sit upright again, the sight of the gaping hole in the side of his fishing boat and how on earth they were ever going to repair it and get off that godforsaken island became the topic of conversation among them—all except Ludlow.

CHAPTER 35

There is an expression among fairies: A bad penny always turns up. This is also a human expression, and there has been some debate about who used it first, but only among the fairies, since humans don't know fairies use the expression or even exist.

Since fairies don't actually use currency of any kind, it's highly unlikely that they were the first to coin the phrase. In fact, most don't even know what it means. Ludlow did know what it meant, and he considered it as he fingered a tarnished penny he'd found in one of Storey's pockets.

While the others bickered and bantered over their situation, Ludlow stood on the rocky shore, looking back and forth between the hole in the side of the fishing boat and the horizon.

"A bad penny," he said to himself, releasing the coin.

"She'll just keep turning up."

Raghnall scurried about on the deck of the fishing boat, gathering supplies as he went. Rope and tools and objects Ludlow had never seen before were flung over the side of the grounded boat and landed in puddles and the wet sand.

"Wait, what's he up to now?" Harry asked, as she settled on Ludlow's shoulder.

"I haven't been listening, but I reckon he's going to try to repair the hole," Ludlow answered.

"What with?" Harry asked.

"No idea," Ludlow answered.

"Have you got any tar?" Raghnall called down to Storey, who was sitting on the beach with his back against a large rock.

"Tar?" Storey shouted back, though it turned into a cough before he asked again. "Tar? No, of course not."

"No bother. I'll find something else," he said, disappearing from the deck and reappearing in the middle of the hole to stretch a measuring tape across it.

"Do you seriously think you can repair this hole?" Storey asked. "I mean, look at the size of it. It must be a meter across and just as high."

"Almost," Raghnall said. "You humans do exaggerate. Compared to the holes I've repaired on the *Anathema*, this is barely a dent."

"Barely a dent?" Storey repeated, finally struggling to his feet.

"I'll have it sorted by morning," Raghnall said, and disappeared again, while Storey paced the beach in front of the hole, muttering inaudibly to himself except for the occasional "dent" and "morning" and "madness." Duchess followed close behind him at first, but eventually she gave up following him nowhere and lay down in the sand and watched.

"Will she ever leave?" Harry asked.

"Duchess?" Ludlow asked.

"No," Harry said.

"Morag?" he tried again.

"No."

"Who then?" he asked.

"Who, indeed? That mermaid," she huffed. "Every time I turn around, there she is."

Isla shrieked as a metal tool box splashed down into the shallow water beside her.

"Could you fetch that tool box for us?" Raghnall called down to her from the deck, and Isla quickly dipped below the surface to retrieve it.

"Lucky for us she doesn't leave," Ludlow answered. "She's rescued every one of us already, maybe more than once."

"I don't buy it," Harry said. "She's up to something."

"Like what?"

"Well, how does Morag keep tracking us down?" Harry asked, as Isla reappeared with the dripping tool box. "I'll tell you. Little Miss Clever-fins over there splish-splashes off and tells her where we are, Morag rains down some earth-quaking wails on us and then Miss Clever-fins comes to our rescue and everyone sings her praises."

"That's ridiculous," Ludlow said. Harry breathed in a deep breath and raised a finger, no doubt about to make another stunning accusation, but was brushed away by Ludlow's own fingers before she could get one more word out.

"I'm going for a walk," he said.

The island had been quite drenched by the storm. The muddy sand seemed to be trying to suck Ludlow's feet in with every step, and the footprints he left behind instantly filled with water. It was an oddly shaped island, the beach twisting and turning so that when he looked back one moment he had a perfect view of his companions, and the next moment they were nowhere to be seen, as if he were totally alone. He stopped in one such place and looked out at the horizon, for what, he didn't know: Morag's ship or any ship or another sea monster or creature from a story book. He plopped down onto the muddy shore and pulled off his shoes one at a time, pulled his trousers up above his knees and looked down at his scratched and bruised legs and cried. He hugged his shoes as if they were his teddy bear and cried into the muddy laces. When the tears finally stopped falling, he dried his cheeks with one sleeve of his oversized t-shirt, then the other, then a wet snout.

He opened his eyes to see that he had been surrounded by grey seals, and one in particular was licking his face. He scurried backwards away from it, but it shuffled up to him once more.

"Are you really seals?" Ludlow asked.

There was no answer from the seals, only tilted heads and curious expressions, because they were really seals.

"I mean, you're not actually sea monsters or some figment of my imagination?" Ludlow asked.

They continued to gather around him, nudging him with their long snouts and sniffing him as animals do, until one by one they all seemed to decide it was time for a good rest and flopped down into the sand around him to bask in the warmth of the sun. It was quite awkward at first, and Ludlow squirmed slightly to get comfortable and to keep his left foot from being crushed, but eventually he gave in and sank back into the pile of seals as if it were a bed covered in soft coats. He closed his eyes and lay awhile among the beached animals, warm and comforted, until a familiar fluttering caught his ear. He slowly opened his eyes to the deep blue sky, empty but for the sun slowly sinking in the west and, eventually, a rather annoying fairy, darting back and forth willy-nilly above him.

"Ludlow!" she shouted, landing on the head of a seal. "What have you done with him you great, hulking beast?"

He appeared from under a mound of blubbery seals, a few of them snorting in discomfort as he did, and shouted back at her.

"What do you want?"

"Oh, there you are. Come along now. Storey has a plan," she answered, and flitted quickly back along the shoreline and out of sight.

Ludlow wriggled his way through the seals, stopping in a vacant plot of sand to pull his shoes back on. He tugged at a lace that was knotted and caked in mud.

"What are those?" Isla asked.

He jolted with fright. "My God!" he shouted. "You scared me half to death."

Isla lay in the surf, propped up on her elbows, her tail flicking in the foamy seawater, the waves washing up around her and trickling away again.

"Are they like shells?" she asked, looking at his shoes.

"Oh," Ludlow said, "well, they protect your feet."

"So they *are* like shells," she said.

"Yeah," he said, "I guess they are."

"Human shells," she said, smiling at him.

"Hey," he asked, "how did you know about rescue breaths?" He finally got his laces untied and one shoe pulled on. She didn't respond at first, she only looked at him blankly. "What Raghnall did," he said. "Mouth-to-mouth respiration I think it's called."

"Oh, well," she said, "we mermaids are no strangers to drownings and disasters at sea. My father can actually sense when one is about to happen. He used to try to warn folk, but then humans started believing we were causing them, and…" she paused. You know the rest of this story, but apparently Isla couldn't bring herself to tell it. "Well, we're forbidden to approach humans now."

"So why do you keep helping me?" Ludlow asked.

She only curled the corner of her mouth and shrugged her shoulders in response, while he struggled to get his shoe tied.

"I've never seen a human as small as you," she said.

"Thanks for noticing," he grumbled.

"Are you a child, like me?" she asked.

"Oh," he said, realizing she hadn't been insulting him. "Yes. I'm eleven years old."

"That's quite young for a human, isn't it?" she asked. "To be at sea without his parents."

"It is," Ludlow answered, pulling on his second shoe.

"So where are your parents? How did you end up here?" she asked.

Ludlow sat looking at her enquiring face as a deep

sadness came over him. He suddenly shuddered with cold, even though the sun was shining high above them and the air was quite warm and comforting.

"I don't remember," he said, quietly.

"You don't remember?" she asked.

"No. I sort of remember bits and pieces—it was my birthday, it was pouring rain, there were people at my house, and then I was in a packing crate," he said.

"A packing crate?" she asked. "What in the world is a packing crate?"

"It's just a large wooden box," he said.

"How did you end up in a large wooden box?"

"I don't remember," he said again.

"Don't remember?" she asked. "Were you struck on the head?"

"I don't know. Harry said I'd remember," he said.

Isla kept talking, but Ludlow had stopped listening. A tightness grew in his chest and another tear welled up in the corner of his eye. Her voice sounded far away, as though coming from another room behind a closed door. He grasped at memories as he stared down at his wet shoes.

"I only remember feeling sad," Ludlow said, interrupting

her.

"Well," she said, "there is another possibility."

"I don't think I've ever been so sad," he said, as Isla went on.

"My father says sometimes creatures can't remember things because they don't really want to."

CHAPTER 36

As Ludlow approached his friends on the beach, he didn't have much hope for Storey's plan, and when he heard it being discussed, he had even less.

"Look, we'll just cover it up for the night so she doesn't spot it and we'll find somewhere to sleep farther inland," Storey said, his arms overflowing with blankets.

"But I'm almost done," Raghnall argued, and he was. In the short time Ludlow had been gone, Raghnall had almost completely patched the hole. If it hadn't been for the metal pulls, and the sheets and blankets strewn about the beach, Ludlow would have never suspected the planks had formerly been dresser drawers. "I just have to find something to seal it with. I can get it finished, I'm sure I can."

"Are we going to find something to seal it with before

dark? Before the tides come in? Really?" Storey asked.

"Are you sure you haven't got any tar?" Raghnall asked.

"Positive," he answered.

"Then I guess we should sleep on it," Raghnall agreed.

"Right, exactly, and we'll figure out how to seal it and shove off in the morning," Storey said, sighing with relief for a moment.

"That's the plan?" Ludlow asked, as Harry landed on his shoulder.

"Not more arguments," Storey said. "I've just been through this with these two. Now look here, I've had just about the most bizarre and unpleasant day of my entire life."

"That must be quite a long time," Raghnall said.

"Yes, and thank you for pointing that out. I've also almost been killed, and I'd really just like to have a good night's rest."

"We don't have time to rest," Ludlow said. "We have to come up with a plan, a proper plan."

"Enough arguing," Storey said. "Who's the oldest person here? Hmm?"

"I don't know how old I am," Raghnall said.

"I'm a hundred and five," Harry answered.

"A hundred and five?" Storey asked. "Really?"

"No," she answered.

"Look," Storey said, and after taking a few deep breaths, "we have a plan. The plan is to anchor the boat, camouflage it as best we can before the tides come in, find somewhere inland to spend the night before dark, get a map out and figure out where we are, then, in the morning, bail out the boat and finish repairing it so we can get back on a course to England."

"She'll come back, though," Ludlow said. "She'll come back and she'll keep coming. She'll keep turning up like a bad penny."

"A bad penny?" Storey repeated.

"What will we do when we get to England?" Ludlow asked. "Call the police? Tell them a banshee's coming after us?" and before Storey could answer him, he continued. "Even if she doesn't," he said, "she'll kidnap another child. I'm sure of it."

Storey held his head in his hands and looked at each of them, once and then again. "Alright," he finally said. "We'll rest for the night, get our bearings, and tomorrow morning we'll come up with a better plan. I promise."

"A plan to defeat her," Ludlow said.

"A plan to defeat a banshee, yes," Storey said. "If there is such a thing."

It isn't easy to come up with a plan to defeat a banshee. For one thing, they have an overwhelming survival instinct. For another, if you upset them in any way, they are liable to start keening and kill you first without even really trying. You could sneak up on one with a big stick in your hand and try to catch her unaware, and as soon as she saw you and let out a wail, the stick would snap in two and you would be knocked out instead of her.

It is possible to kill a banshee, though. Even the goblins, with their short memories and constant bickering, had managed to figure out at least one way.

As they gathered palm fronds and driftwood from the beach to cover the fishing boat, Ludlow tried to come up with a plan. He thought about it until he could think of nothing else, not even what he was meant to be doing.

"Are you okay, Lud?" Raghnall asked.

"What do you mean?" Ludlow asked.

"Well, you've been walking back and forth with that

same branch for nearly ten minutes now. I just wondered whether you were ever going to put it over the boat."

"Oh," Ludlow replied. "I hadn't even noticed."

Raghnall took the branch from his hand and leaned in to whisper, "We had a plan, you know? The goblins did. To get rid of her."

"I know," Ludlow answered. "Harry told me."

"Harry knew about it?" Raghnall asked.

Ludlow shrugged.

"Well, why doesn't she just tell us what it was?"

Ludlow shrugged again.

"Where is she anyway?" Raghnall asked. "One minute she's here and the next, she's gone."

"Who is?" she asked, appearing behind them.

"You. Where were you?" Raghnall asked.

"Looking for a place to set up camp for the night. Why?" she asked.

"Never mind that. What's this about you knowing the goblins' plan to get rid of Morag?"

"Well, you never told me what it was," she said.

"No, I reckon we were smart enough to leave you out of it," he said.

"Too bad you weren't smart enough to remember it," she replied, before turning and flickering off up the hill again. They watched the light of her disappear into the trees and reappear in a clearing before Storey walked by, dragging a bushel of palm fronds.

"Your little girlfriends do have a habit of disappearing and reappearing, don't they?" Storey asked, as he passed.

"They're not my girlfriends," Ludlow said.

"No," Storey said. "They're not even girls are they? I suppose I'm lucky they aren't."

"Why's that?" Raghnall asked.

"Well if it weren't for that mermaid, I'd have drowned today," Storey said. "No human could've fished me out of the drink like that. When we get back to England, I really ought to learn how to swim."

"You can't swim?" Ludlow asked. "You spend your life on a boat and you can't swim?"

Sometimes, something happens that triggers a goblin's memory, just the way it does for human beings.

"Say that again," Raghnall said.

"Say what again?" Ludlow asked. "Can't swim?"

"That's right," Raghnall said. "Can't swim," he said, and

then, as if he had just had the most important thought of his entire life, he said it again, almost shouting with glee, "Can't swim!"

CHAPTER 37

Goblins are actually rather carefree, live-and-let-live type of creatures under ordinary circumstances. It wouldn't normally cross a goblin's mind to assist in the kidnapping of a human child from their own home. As Raghnall recounted, on their occasional days off, the goblin crew of the *Anathema* had spent their time mooring near uninhabited islands and mucking about in the sea, or building tree houses on the shore and making believe they were pirates in search of buried treasure and ingredients that the ever-popular dish of slop could be made from. The plan, therefore, which Raghnall now finally remembered, had been to moor close enough to an island that they could reach it in the lifeboats and rig the ship to sink with Morag on it. Banshees, they'd discovered, being land bound creatures, can't swim, and goblins would be more than happy to spend the rest of their days marooned and eating slop on a beach.

"So one of us gets aboard, rigs the gunpowder barrels to explode and gets off in time not to die in the explosion, is that it?" Storey asked, as he served Raghnall a slice of cold pork pie.

Harry had found quite a comfortable spot for them to settle down in for the night: a little clearing on the hillside, swept over with long soft grass, from which they had a perfect view of the horizon and beach, and a little island of branches and palms that used to be the *Lyonesse*. They sat around a blanket, discussing the plan and feasting on the food Storey had brought with him: cold pork and parsnip pie, leftover boiled potatoes with chive cream, sardines, cheddar cheese, hard boiled eggs, pickled yellow string beans and beets, ripe garden tomatoes, soda bread and butter, scones, clotted cream, strawberry-rhubarb jam and chocolate dipped shortbread cookies, along with the last of Raghnall's orange cream-filled dark chocolates and a tin of dog food. Though Raghnall and Harry both tried the dog food, they only tried it once.

"The barrels are already rigged," Raghnall answered,

his mouth full of scone. "The fuse just has to be lit."

"Why exactly is the ship carrying rigged barrels of gunpowder?" Storey asked, serving a slice of pie to Ludlow.

"I don't know, actually," Raghnall answered. "They were there when I came aboard. I think it might have been a pirate ship once. It's a tall ship. Could be hundreds of years old."

"Alright then," Storey began, seeming to think it through as he spoke, "tomorrow morning, Harry will track down the mermaid..."

"I'll do no such thing," Harry said.

"Harry," Raghnall said with a sigh.

"I won't," she said.

"It's our only chance, Harry," Ludlow said.

"Fine," she answered, "but I don't like this one bit. That mermaid is trouble," she insisted, before stuffing a hunk of cheese into her mouth.

"So," Storey went on, "she'll track down the mermaid and bring her back to the beach, we'll uncover the boat we've just spent the better part of the evening covering up, and when Morbid spots it and gets close enough, the mermaid will swim me out to the ship, I'll sneak on, light the fuse…"

"Once the goblins are off the ship, you mean," Raghnall interrupted.

"I'm sorry?" Storey asked. "On top of everything, I've got to look out for the goblins that have helped her try to kill us? Twice?"

"Yes, please," Raghnall nodded.

Storey looked into his pleading eyes. "Raghnall?" he asked. "Were your eyes blue when I met you?"

"No, sir," he answered, "My eyes are hazel-brown," he said, tilting his knife and looking into it as a mirror.

"I noticed that too," Ludlow said.

"That's very curious, isn't it?" Raghnall asked.

"Everything about this day has been curious," Storey said. "It's just one curious event after another." He shook his head. "Fine, let's figure a way to get these goblins off the ship."

"We don't have to," Raghnall said. "She'll send them ashore on the lifeboats. She won't leave the ship herself. She's too afraid of falling into the sea."

"And she's usually happy to be rid of the crew, truth be told," Harry added.

"So, you're sure she'll be alone?" Storey asked. "All of your little friends will be off the ship?"

"Well, I don't know if I'd call them my friends, but they don't generally mean anyone any harm…"

"Yes, right, but they'll all be off the ship?" Storey asked again.

"Should be. Yes, sir," Raghnall nodded.

"Right, so we have a plan. Now all we need are some matches we don't have," he said, shaking his head and pitching his pork pie crust into his plate, as Ludlow reached into the pocket of his huge cut-off trousers and pulled out the little metal canister.

"We do have matches," he said.

"Eh?" Storey's forehead wrinkled. "What else have you got in there?"

"A compass and a pocket telescope," Ludlow answered.

"Curiouser and curiouser all the time," Storey said. "Well, let's finish up our meal and get some sleep. I've a big day ahead of me tomorrow."

There had been some talk of starting a campfire until Storey pointed out it would attract attention, and Raghnall noted it would be dangerous to fall asleep next to an open flame, and Harry reminded them all that the banshee on their tails could turn a campfire into a ravaging forest fire with just one conjuring wail.

Instead, they made a big bed out of all of Storey's dry clothes and the towels and blankets from the fishing boat, and nestled in around Duchess for a good night's sleep—all except Ludlow.

Ludlow had no intention of sleeping. His plan was different from the others' plan, almost identical, except in one small detail; in Ludlow's plan, he was the one to sneak back aboard the ship. He just had to figure out how to do it. He thought and thought. He thought with one finger against his forehead, then with his fingers pressed into the sides of his head, then with his whole head in his hands, but it was futile. There was no way he could get to the ship without Isla, no way his own smaller-than-average eleven-year-old arms could swim him all the way out to the deep water and no boat to carry him.

Just when he thought it was hopeless and that he might as well forget the whole idea and go to sleep like the others, he saw a flicker on the horizon. His eyes were growing heavy, but he watched it. It grew and grew and split into four flickers on the water, with three of them moving ever closer while the other stayed moored out in the deep. Morag had already found them. He didn't know how she'd done it, but she had. Three newly patched lifeboats filled with goblins were advancing on the island in the dark. Ludlow reached into his pocket and pulled out the telescope to get a better view. Through the scope he saw the first lifeboat stop beside the camouflaged fishing boat; one goblin grabbed a lantern and the others followed him onto the deck.

Ludlow turned to his companions, all fast asleep and snoring loudly, and finally had a plan. He pulled the alarm clock from the burlap sack, wound and set it to go off fifteen minutes later, and tucked it into the crook of Raghnall's arm. He would be long gone by the time it went off and alerted his friends.

As he emerged from the shadow of the trees onto the moonlit beach, the other two lifeboats ploughed into the shore, with all of the goblins abandoning the boats and scattering into the trees and along the beach in the opposite direction. Apart from one goblin who was quite interested to know whether slop could be made from a coconut, they were all so preoccupied with their search that not a single one of them noticed a human child making off with one of their empty lifeboats.

That's not to say, though, that no one noticed.

CHAPTER 38

The rowing of the lifeboat, which Ludlow had expected would be the trickiest part of his new plan, turned out not to be. It was, indeed, difficult to stay on course, facing away from the *Anathema* with only a hint of moonlight reaching the compass on his lap. The trickiest part was, in fact, that he couldn't figure out a way to get from the lifeboat onto the deck of the ship. He rowed around the entire ship before he finally accepted that the only way up was to climb the huge chain linked to the anchor. He tied the lifeboat to it as best he could and checked his pocket to make sure he still had the matches before attempting the climb, and a long and difficult ascent it would prove to be.

His hands slipped on the slick metal links, and it took him a few minutes to climb even a short distance. He stopped to catch his breath and looked back at the island.

The air was cool and still and quiet, until...

"What are you doing, Ludlow Osgoode?" she asked from beneath him. Ludlow nearly lost his grip at the sound of her voice. When he'd wrapped his arms tightly around the chain once more, he looked up for Morag and then down to see Isla, hugging the edge of the lifeboat, her chin resting on her folded arms. He wondered how long she'd been down there, watching.

"What are you doing here?" he whispered.

"Watching you," she said.

"Keep your voice down, please," Ludlow whispered.

"Why?" she whispered back. "Are you surprising someone?"

"Something like that," he answered. "Anyway, you didn't answer me. What are you doing here? Don't mermaids sleep at night?"

"Yes," she answered. "Don't humans sleep at night?" she asked.

"Well, yes, but I'm trying to...surprise someone," he said.

"I love surprises," she said. "Is it someone's birthday?" she asked.

"No," he answered as he reached up to continue his climb.

"What is this ship?" she asked.

"You don't know?" he asked over his shoulder.

"No," she shook her head. "Should I?"

"You still haven't answered my question," Ludlow said. "What are you doing here?"

"Father had a feeling...there was going to be a shipwreck," she said, and Ludlow stopped again and looked down at her. She lowered her eyes and started twirling a long, wet strand of hair around her finger. "And I was worried about you. This is the ship, isn't it? The banshee's ship?"

He nodded.

"What are you going to do?" she asked.

"You should go, Isla," he said. "Couldn't you get in a lot of trouble for being here?"

She nodded.

"Well then?"

"Where are the others?" she asked.

"They...couldn't come," he answered.

"Really?" she asked, a tremor in her voice. "Maybe you

think I'm just a silly mermaid, but I think you're a silly boy. I've seen what she can do. Do you think you're going to defeat her on your own?"

"You don't think I could?"

"I think you don't *have* to. That's not the same thing."

"She's after me, Isla," he said. "Me. She told me she'd come after me. I put Raghnall, Harry and Storey in danger. I can't hide from my troubles anymore. I have to face her."

"But you don't have to do it alone," she said. "You're the most wonderful human boy I've ever met..." she started.

"Aren't I the only human boy you've ever met?" he asked.

"...and those creatures all care for you and want to help you," she continued. Ludlow shook his head and reached up to loop his hand into another chain link. He was getting the hang of it now. After a few minutes of climbing he was almost at the top, but not too far from the water to hear Isla say, "You're the silliest human boy I've ever met," and to look down and watch her sink back into the sea.

CHAPTER 39

Peering over the side, he saw no sign of Morag. He gave another long look around, and a long listen, and then threw himself over the side and onto the forecastle.

He peeked into his pocket to make sure he hadn't dropped the matches as a dim light skimmed over the deck beside him and dropped onto the upper deck, out of view.

Harry, he thought, but it couldn't have been.

Ludlow slinked along the forecastle and stopped dead at the top of the stairs. There stood Morag at the bottom, her back to him, facing the island. Ludlow ducked behind a coil of rope and watched her. She stood between Ludlow and the hatch, glowing an eerie green whenever the moon was obscured by clouds. She was deathly still; only wisps of her shroud and creeping vines of hair rustled in the gentle wind.

He crouched there for so long that his legs began to tremble, and with a few rocks of the ship he had fallen backwards onto his back. He lay there, motionless, hoping she hadn't heard him.

"Finally," he suddenly heard her say. "What took you so long?"

She wasn't talking to him. Who was she talking to? *Someone's returned to the ship*, he thought. He held his breath and strained his ears to hear their answer, but the next voice he heard was still Morag's.

"Well, where is the human child?"

He heard a whisper and then footsteps crossing the deck, and the door to Morag's quarters slammed shut. He had no time to spare. He jumped to his feet and pounced down the stairs on the tips of his toes. He heard raised voices from inside the captain's quarters as he raced across the upper deck, skidding through puddles of water and flailing his arms to steady himself as he did.

He slid into the frame of the hatch, stubbing the same toe he had stubbed before, because that's just always the way, but at least it stopped him from falling in and down the stairs; the hatch was open wide. After briefly clutching the tips of his toes and wincing in pain, he stood upright again and stared into the darkness. Wishing Harry had been there to light the way or that he was less afraid of the dark, he stood frozen, unable to take a step into the dark hole. He felt his pocket for the tube of matches, but as he did, a commotion arose from the beach, and the sound of anxious footsteps grew from within Morag's quarters, and the dark didn't seem so frightening anymore.

He bounded down one step, two, four, seven, the darkness ever deepening, until the tenth step, when a cold draft swept down from the top of the stairs and a lantern sparked to life on the wall beside him. You may think that strange, and so did Ludlow, but nevertheless he grabbed it and quickly continued down the stairs and made his way to the storage room.

The door was open. He narrowly avoided tripping over the large glass jar as he rushed the barrels of gunpowder. They were no longer rigged to explode, the way he remembered and the way Raghnall had described. There was no time to wonder why, though, and Ludlow quickly busied himself by dipping one end of the cord into the biggest barrel and wrapping as many barrels as he could. It took him much longer than he thought it would. It seemed as though it took him longer to wrap each barrel than it had taken to wrap the last. He started to feel unusually heavy as he wrapped the final barrel. His arms seemed to be falling asleep. He stopped and shook them before reaching into the pocket of his trousers and pulling out the tube of matches. He struggled with the lid again, which was now almost completely rusted shut and caked with salt. When he finally got it open, he nudged one match slowly up and out with his fingertip. He yawned. The match felt heavy. He dragged the tip against the lid of a barrel, too slowly. It didn't light. He tried again, managing a spark this time. The third time, it lit with a sizzle. He stood staring at the flame, watching it flash and flicker, and then looked over at the end of the rope. All he had to do was light it, and run. As he lowered the match towards the frayed end, it was quickly snuffed out by another sudden, icy cold draft. He dropped the spent match on the ground, but instead of pulling out another match, he found himself screwing the lid back onto the tube. He yawned as he slipped the tube back into his pocket and backed slowly out of the room. Suddenly, he was so tired, so heavy, so limp, that all he wanted to do was find a place to sit down.

He stumbled across the lower deck, past the staircase to a little chair; a little, familiar looking chair. It looked just like the antique chair in the front hall of his house. He slumped backwards into it and closed his eyes, just for a moment, and when he opened them again, though his vision was a bit blurry, he could see that he was back home, sitting in that same chair, right where his father had left him.

Toby went trotting past him, back to the frosted glass door, where he waited every day for Ludlow's grandmother to come home from her errands and take him for his walk. The hall was still piled high with fallen rain boots and cluttered with dripping umbrellas, and the rack on the wall still overflowed with dark-coloured coats.

The hall was empty except for Toby and Ludlow. He slid off of the chair and started walking towards the kitchen, where his mother and father surely were, but when he reached the open door to the spare room, he couldn't help but linger there. As he peered in, his chest tightened and grew heavy, though not in the same way as the rest of his body. The bed was piled high with his grandmother's old coats. His parents had already started to pack up her belongings. He slipped in and quietly closed the door behind him. He rubbed his eyes, which were caked with dried tears, and drifted into the room, meandering between the scattered boxes until he reached the bed. He snuggled into the woolen and fur coats and breathed in the smells of perfume and moth balls. He rubbed his cheeks against the soft fur of a mink coat. His mother hated furs, but said old coats like these shouldn't be wasted, and someone else could use them, but he didn't want her to give them away. He didn't want any of her things given away; they were his nana's. He heard footsteps and voices in the hall, his father and uncle, from the sound of them, and he pulled the coats over himself to hide. He was quite content to hide under her coats, warm and comforted, and planned to spend the remainder of the day there, until...

"Sweetheart," she said. He froze. He didn't blink or breathe. He listened for a moment, trying to hear her voice again. He thought he was losing his mind. After all, moments ago he had thought he was on a ship, hiding from a banshee.

"I'm going crazy," he whispered.

"What was that?" she asked. Ludlow bolted upright in the bed and pushed away the coats. The door to the closet was ajar. He was sure her voice had come from within it.

"Nana?" he whispered.

"Hmm?" he heard her voice again. "Oh, I was just saying I'll finish sorting through these things in here, and then I'm going round to the shops. Would you like to come? We could stop in at the sweet shop and get you something if you like."

"Oh, yes please," Ludlow answered as he leapt down from the bed and ran to the closet door. "At Beattie's Sweeties. Beattie's Special Dark Choc-orange Creams please, Nana," he said, as he pulled the door wide to reveal not his grandmother but a fairy.

"Sorry," Harry said, pulling her fingers away from her temples. "Not Nana."

He opened his mouth to cry out, but instead he yawned. His eyes pulled closed, weighted down with sleep, and everything went black.

His body jerked, as your body sometimes does when you're having a nightmare of falling or being chased, and when his eyes opened again he found himself lying on the damp, dirty floor of the ship's lower deck, with both Morag and Harry towering over him, glowing blindingly against the darkness.

"I cannot believe you fell for that again," Morag said. "Stupid human."

As you may recall, Harry had the ability to alter human beings' perceptions of creatures, places and time.

"Harry?" Ludlow asked, trying to focus.

"Do you remember the trick now?" she asked.

He did remember the trick, and everything that had come before: that his grandmother had died, that they'd spent his eleventh birthday at her funeral, and that he'd been trying to hide from his troubles under a pile of coats in her bedroom when he was lured by Harry. Of course, you know the rest.

"I tried to tell you it worked best on the grieving," Harry said. "I told you you'd got yourself into this. I told you you'd remember."

Another important thing to know about Ludlow, is how much he loved his grandmother. It is hard to measure one person's love for another, but he easily loved her more than banshees love numbers or revenge, more than fairies love themselves and more than goblins love eating slop and mucking about on a beach, and she was gone.

"I remember," he said, staring past them into the deep darkness. "I remember everything."

CHAPTER 40

"What was the plan then, child?" Morag asked. "To blow up the ship? Well, you must think yourself very clever. Very clever, indeed, but did you think you were the first to devise such a plan?"

"It wasn't entirely my plan," he answered, still lying on the floor. He couldn't move.

"Whoever devised it, I assure you, he was not the first," she said, a wicked grin spreading across her lips. "Because I was."

"What?" Ludlow asked.

"You heard her," Harry said, and then, "Wait, what?" she asked Morag.

"Did you think it was just luck that this ship was carrying barrels of gunpowder rigged to explode? That was my plan all along. To rid the world of you snivelling little beasts, even if only a few. Selfish, ungrateful brats," she said, almost to herself.

"What snivelling little beasts?" Ludlow asked.

"Human children, of course. What other kind of snivelling little beast could you be?" she asked.

"You said you loved children," Harry said.

"I say a lot of things," Morag said. "Some are true, others not."

"What else have you lied to me about?" Harry asked.

"Oh, a great number of things—how I died, how I came to be captain of this ship, what happened to that infernal little beast of a girl who was lugging you about in a jar," she answered. "What did she call you? *Fairae* Obnoxious?"

Harry's eyes and mouth opened wide.

"Why do you seem so surprised? You know I lied about letting you go once you brought me Twenty-four."

"What about your own child?" Ludlow asked.

"You had a child?" Harry asked.

"Was that a lie too?" Ludlow asked.

"No," Morag answered. "Sadly, that was true. James—a horrible little beast he was. In fact, if it were not for him you would not even be here."

"How can that be?" Harry asked.

"Because he killed me."

One final thing you should know about banshees is that not all banshees started out that way. Some, like Morag, started out as human beings.

"Bringing that child into this world killed me," Morag explained. "I died in childbirth, at the tender age of twenty-five years, yet he lives happily, with my husband and family. He made me what I am, and he lives..." her voice trailed off as she stared into a dark corner of the lower deck. "When I awakened as a banshee, they were gone," she went on. "They had left my gravesite, left our home, our town. I never found them, and so I devised a plan—to kill twenty-five children. Revenge for one killing me," she said, finally looking back at him.

"What about the crew?" Ludlow asked.

"The crew," she said, shaking her head. "What of them? Do you think I care anything for the fate of those imbeciles? They are just as bad as human children, if not worse. Of all the banshee curses with which I could have been saddled it was that—to be forever surrounded by goblins," she said.

"That was your curse?" Harry asked.

"I just needed one more child. One more and every berth would have been filled. Twenty-five. Not now, though. Now, I will have to get Raghnall back, and Harry will have to help me kidnap two more children."

"Two more?" Harry asked.

"That is correct," Morag answered. "We will be short two after tonight."

"Why two?" Harry asked.

Morag extended her open hand towards Ludlow. "The matches," she said.

He slipped his hand into his pocket and closed his fist around the canister.

"The matches. Give them to me!" she shouted, grabbing his arm and pulling him to his feet. She was unnaturally strong. She pulled his hand out of his pocket and pried his fingers away from the metal cylinder one by one until she had it, and dragged him struggling back up the stairs to the upper deck, with Harry following close behind.

"My matches," she said, looking at the canister in the moonlight. "Stolen from my quarters. Little beast."

"I won't do it," Harry said, suddenly.

"What will you not do?" Morag asked.

"Help you kidnap more children," Harry said.

"I had no trouble luring children before you came aboard," Morag said. "You will either help me or meet the same fate as Twenty-four," Morag said. "Now take these away," Morag ordered, thrusting her arm back and shoving the matches into Harry's open arms.

"Wait, same fate? What do you mean? What are you going to do to him?" Harry asked, as the racket that arose from the beach grew so loud Morag couldn't ignore it anymore. There were shouts and cries, the words were unclear, but when they turned to look to the shore they saw that one of the lifeboats had been set alight.

"What is going on over there?" Morag asked. "Confounded creatures. Cursed creatures. Maddening. The boy is not even there. All they have to do is bring back Raghnall. How difficult could that be?" she asked.

"Raghnall won't come willingly," Ludlow said, "and he's not alone."

"Not alone?" Morag asked. "What do you mean? Who is with him?"

Ludlow realized that perhaps he shouldn't say any more, so when he wouldn't answer, Morag looked to Harry.

"What is the boy talking about?" she asked.

"Well, there's the fisherman," Harry started.

"The fisherman," Morag said. "He lives? I was sure he would have had a heart attack or drowned by now."

"And there's the mermaid," Harry continued.

"A mermaid?" Morag asked.

"Wait, you didn't know about the mermaid?" Ludlow asked, although he didn't need to hear the answer. In that instant he finally understood, and then looking at Harry he asked, "It's been you this whole time? You've been signalling her? You tried to put the blame on Isla."

"Who is Isla?" Morag asked.

"I just wanted us to be together," Harry said. "You were going to leave me behind when you got to England."

"I thought you were my friend!" Ludlow shouted.

"I am your friend," she said, hugging the tube of matches.

"A friend wouldn't have done what you did," Ludlow said. "You're not my friend."

It's extremely rare for a human to break a fairy's heart for one simple reason: fairies almost never care enough about a human to have their hearts broken by one. It does happen, though.

"I only did it so you wouldn't leave me," Harry said.

"Enough of this," Morag said, and continued to drag Ludlow to the stern of the ship.

"We could stay here, on the ship, and be friends," Harry said.

"Stay on the ship? Didn't you...hear her?" Ludlow asked, struggling to free himself. "She's going to...blow the ship up herself."

"Say your goodbyes, Adhair," Morag said.

"What? No. Why?" Harry asked, still clutching the tube of matches.

"Because after tonight," Morag said, pushing him in front of her and lifting him up onto the railing, "you will never see this snivelling little beast again."

He teetered on the edge, looking down into the deep, dark water.

"No!" Harry shouted.

Ludlow turned back to look at her, but she had vanished.

"We will find more children. Unfortunately, there are millions more of you," Morag said. That is when eleven-year-old Ludlow Osgoode, who was quite small for his age, fought a wailing banshee.

The first swing of his arm went right through her ghostly form, but the second made contact and knocked her sideways. When she landed on her back, Ludlow jumped down from the railing and tried to run back to the hatch, but she grabbed him by the ankle. He fell face-first onto the deck. It knocked the wind out of him, but he was quickly on his knees and trying to shake her off. He looked back as he kicked wildly, almost breaking free from her, until he noticed a purple flicker in her eyes as her mouth opened wide.

"No!" he shouted. He fell back and threw his hands over her mouth and then his whole chest over her face. She struggled beneath him at first, but then she calmed and seemed to even be laughing into his open hands when her arms came up around him and she rose, almost effortlessly, from the deck. When she pulled him away from her face he realized she was, indeed, laughing, and when she hoisted him back up onto the railing, he knew why. She hadn't been about to wail. He'd been tricked again, but this time Ludlow thought he had a trick of his own.

"Go on then," he said. "Drop me."

Morag stared at him, her brow furrowed.

"The mermaid will rescue me," he said.

Morag eyed him for a moment more and then leaned over the railing to look down into the dark water.

"But she won't rescue you," he said, as he grabbed her knotted hair and jumped from the ship, pulling her down with him.

The water was icy cold; at first it stung his skin, but his body quickly began to numb. He eventually rose to the surface, with Morag following shortly after him. She struggled violently to stay afloat as Ludlow swam clumsily back towards the lifeboat. There was no sign of Isla; he would have to save himself. Though he couldn't feel his arms and legs moving through the water, they were moving. He was almost there.

"You are not winning this battle!" Morag shouted, spitting salt water.

"Neither...are you," Ludlow gasped and wheezed, "and that's...good enough...for me."

As you may recall, unless caught completely by surprise, it is extremely difficult (bordering on the impossible) to kill a banshee. Given an opportunity to wail, they have an arsenal of weapons at their disposal. As Ludlow finally grabbed onto the edge of the lifeboat, he noticed that Morag had stopped struggling. The splashing and sputtering had completely ceased. He thought she must have finally drowned, until he heard the sound.

CHAPTER 41

This time, the wail was so piercingly high-pitched, so shatteringly shrill that it cracked the panes of glass throughout the ship above him. Ludlow clambered into the lifeboat and crouched, trembling on the floor, waiting to be tossed about by a raging sea or the wind of a storm or both, but he would be waiting for quite some time. Morag's wail hadn't conjured either of those things. Just as he was about to peek over the side of the lifeboat, he heard what sounded like hail pelting into the water but was actually the shattered glass, falling from high above. Ludlow dropped back down, pulling his shirt over his head as shards rained into the boat around him. He opened his eyes to a boatful of glistening glass but wondered how a wail of that magnitude could have resulted only in some broken windows. Once the last shards had fallen, all was quiet—horribly, terribly, unnaturally quiet.

Ludlow sat up cautiously and looked around for Morag. He leaned over the edge of the boat, straining to spot her glow in the dark, when the sea seemed to suddenly drop. *But it couldn't have*, Ludlow thought, *could it?* Just as he thought that, it dropped again. He grabbed the edge of the lifeboat as it dropped a third time and then again. He felt as if his dinner was jumping back up into his throat, over and over. He sat as still as possible, waiting for it to stop. When he was fairly certain it wouldn't happen again, he carefully stood up and readied himself for the long climb back up to the forecastle when, without any warning at all, the lifeboat capsized. He found himself underwater again, being sucked momentarily into an undertow. He fought and struggled against currents that pulled him in opposite directions, until he finally resurfaced.

You would think he would have been relieved that he hadn't yet drowned, and that he was breathing air again, but you would be wrong. The reason he wasn't is because he was, in fact, about twenty meters above the sea and rising, clutched in the clenched fist of a water giant—a phenomenon which is more commonly known as ghost water.

Before you read any further, there are three things you should know about ghost water: (1) it can take many forms but most often takes the shape of a human male; (2) it only manifests as a result of a banshee's wails or at the conjuring of a witch or wizard; and (3) once it's been conjured, it has a mind of its own and no one can control it, not even the one who conjured it.

Its enormous hands had been the first shapes to emerge from the sea. Ludlow looked down to see the top of its head form and then its shoulders and bulging chest. Just when he thought his situation couldn't get any worse, he looked over to see Morag squirming to free herself from the giant's other hand. Then, when he thought his situation was definitely the worst it could possibly be, they were both hurled back onto the deck of the ship.

Ludlow instantly scrambled to his feet, scampering away just in time not to be crushed by the next thing the giant flung against the deck—the lifeboat. It smashed into pieces like a child's toy, within a meter of Ludlow. One of the oars was sent sliding across the deck, and Ludlow chased it down and grabbed it.

When he turned around to face the giant, it was more terrifyingly huge than he had even realized. The ghost water was standing beside the ship—a giant composed entirely of water, standing waist-deep in the sea, its chin higher than the masts of the *Anathema*, its hands the size of small automobiles.

One of its hands was already reaching down for him again. Ludlow swung at it with the oar but only succeeded in splashing water around the deck and irritating the giant. He hadn't by any means deterred it. It continued to grasp at Ludlow as he scurried backwards, ducking behind barrels and crates and jabbing back with the oar, until he finally backed right into Morag's quarters and shut the door tight behind him.

You may be wondering how Ludlow's hiding in the

captain's quarters could keep the ghost water at bay, and the answer is: it really couldn't. It had, however, temporarily confused the ghost water. This didn't prove helpful to Ludlow's situation, though, since the giant began circling the ship in search of him, churning the sea and surrounding the *Anathema* with a wildly swirling whirlpool.

The entire ship began to slant to one side, sending Ludlow stumbling across the floor of Morag's quarters towards the broken windows. He grabbed at a window frame and clung to it, but looking out, he was face to face with the ghost water. That is, until it knocked in the door to Morag's cabin. With one solid blow it had torn through the door, its frame and a great deal of the surrounding wall, and flooded the room with seawater. Every strike after that sent gallons of water into the cabin, rushing past Ludlow and almost pushing him out the window and back into the sea. He knew if he didn't get back onto the outer decks he would drown. He had to convince Morag to stop it. He didn't know she couldn't.

He reached from one window frame to the next, pulling himself towards the gaping hole where the door had once been, and through it he saw Morag, clinging to a railing.

He stumbled out onto the deck, reaching for fixed objects and pulling himself towards her as the ship continued to tilt, spiraling around its anchor. The giant was no longer reaching for either of them, but had rather started batting the ship with its fists as it circled past. Every time it did, a deluge of salty seawater poured down over Ludlow. With his eyes closed tight he tried to grab onto the railing, but when he reached out, what he found was Morag's outstretched hand. When he opened his eyes, he was looking right into hers.

"Make it stop!" Ludlow shouted. "It's going to kill you too!"

"Perhaps it will," she said.

"What about...your plan?" Ludlow asked, spitting out seawater.

"I thought I needed to kill twenty-five," she said, "and I will, if I survive this. In the meantime, I would be content to kill only one." Morag clung to the railing and as the ship continued to tilt, almost onto its side, Ludlow felt the deck slipping away from beneath him and found himself dangling in mid-air. The only thing preventing him from falling into the whirlpool below was Morag's icy grip. He turned his head to look down at the water, but stopped short, his eyes fixed on the hatch to the decks below. A faint light glowed deep within, and Ludlow called out to her.

"Harry!" he shouted. "Harry, if you're really my friend, you know what to do!"

"She is not your friend!" Morag shouted. "Have you not learned that by now? You are alone," she said with a wicked smile, and letting go of her hold on him, sent him plunging into the frigid sea.

As he sank deeper and deeper, pulled by the strong current, the water grew colder and colder, darker and darker, louder and louder and lighter and lighter.

There are three ways to survive ghost water: (1) swimming for your life, which can assist you in: (2) outliving it (ghost water is mightily powerful but has a lifespan of a few hours, at most); or (3) boiling it into oblivion (ghost water is extremely susceptible to heat and therefore, evaporation). This last option, however, isn't usually a viable option at all, since the conditions in open water are not conducive to setting a fire, and especially a fire powerful enough to pose any threat to ghost water. In fact, the only way option three would work is if a ship the size of the *Anathema* exploded right next to it, which was exactly what had happened.

Through the murky water, Ludlow saw the sky above fill with bursts of light, like sparklers on a cake, then fireworks, then explosions, and the surface of the sea was set ablaze. Through it all, though, Ludlow could still make out one tiny, flickering light that fell towards him.

He held his breath for as long as he could, for what seemed like forever and somehow like only seconds. He reached out and grasped at the dimming light, finally grabbing onto it and clutching it to his chest, and just when he couldn't hold his breath any longer, a pair of lips breathed into him and a pair of hands tucked themselves under his arms and lifted him back up to the surface.

As you may recall, Noel D. Adams was one of two people known to have survived ghost water. Ludlow Osgoode was the other. Coincidentally, they were both rescued by a mermaid.

Ludlow gasped loudly as they breached the surface, and choked on the seawater that had seeped into his throat, but soon he was breathing normally again and opening his eyes to see Isla's face smiling a relieved smile, and beyond her, the floating inferno that had once been the *Anathema*. He and Isla clung to each other as they bobbed in the water, watching the masts of the ship surrender and collapse in flames; one in particular crumbled into what had once been the storage room.

"You are my friend after all, Harry," he said quietly.

Not far behind them, among floating, flaming ship debris, was a lifeboat overflowing with goblins and a fisherman, all calling out his name and variations of his name: Laszlo, Ludwig, Leroy, Bill. The goblins had terrible memories, after all.

"Look, there's a human child and a mermaid!" Ludlow heard one shout.

"Maybe that's the human we're looking for," another said, as Ludlow waved them over.

"We're looking for a human?" the first one replied.

"Look, there's a human child and a mermaid," Sully said.

"This is madness," Raghnall said.

"It's enough to drive a perfectly sane person crazy," Storey agreed, as he reached down and pulled Ludlow from Isla's arms and into the crowded lifeboat. "Well done, Lud," he whispered, wrapping him in his raincoat. "Well done."

"Look there!" Raghnall pointed into a cluster of floating wreckage. "A barrel of tar."

CHAPTER 42

Goblins are curious and complex creatures, just as humans are, and there are still a number of important facts about goblins you haven't yet learned. Raghnall said that goblins don't generally mean anyone any harm. While he wasn't wrong, this was an understatement. Goblins can actually be surprisingly generous and helpful, especially when they've been freed from the clutches of a cursed and psychotic banshee. Another important fact about goblins is that the only thing they love more than eating slop is eating strawberry jam, and they will also do almost anything you ask in exchange for a spoonful.

Having been liberated from Morag and provided with not only strawberry jam, but strawberry-rhubarb jam, perhaps the greatest goblin discovery of the century, the goblins of the *Anathema* were making quick work of tarring the patch on the *Lyonesse*. And not just tarring the patch, but polishing the rails and swabbing the deck, which was producing much better results than they had produced on the *Anathema*, since they were now cleaning with fresh rags and a clean mop.

Ludlow sat on the beach, dressed in his own dry clothes once more, wrapped in a blanket and huddled against Duchess as he watched in amazement. They worked in shifts, all twenty-three of them, including Corcoran the oaf, some tending to the *Lyonesse* while others bathed in the sea and washed their clothes.

"Twenty-five," Ludlow said, as Raghnall sat down beside him.

"Twenty-five?" Raghnall asked.

"She had a plan," Ludlow explained, "Morag did, to kidnap and kill twenty-five children."

"Kill twenty-five children?" Raghnall repeated. "How?"

"By blowing up the ship with them on it."

"Where was she going to find twenty-five children?"

"She said she only needed one more," Ludlow said. "It doesn't make sense, does it?"

"No," Raghnall said, shaking his head.

"Fantastic," they heard Storey say. He walked back and forth beside the boat, map under his arm, inspecting the patch. "It's just fantastic."

"They're doing a very good job, aren't they?" Ludlow said.

"The goblins?" Raghnall asked.

"I guess you were right about them," Ludlow said, "but when we saw the fire on the shore, I thought for sure you three were done for."

"Fire?" he asked, and then, "Oh," he said, shaking his head, "that was just goblin forgetfulness. Sully left a lit lantern on one of the lifeboats and then, *poof*. Bit of a panic."

"We'll be off home soon," Storey called to them, a look of slight confusion coupled with pleasant surprise on his face.

"What'll happen to them now?" Ludlow asked.

"Bernie asked me if I was staying with them," Raghnall said. "I think they mean to build shelters and stay on the island. See?" He motioned towards the water's edge, where two goblins were collecting planks and debris from the *Anathema* as they washed up on the shore.

"Oh," Ludlow said with a shiver. "Are you staying with them?"

"I don't know," he said, scratching Duchess behind the ears. "It's strange, but I don't seem to fit in with them anymore," he continued, as Duchess licked his glasses right off his face.

"You could come home with me," Ludlow said. "I mean, I've always thought you'd come home with me. I don't know how to explain you to my mum and dad or anyone," he paused, thinking.

"Where would I stay? Would I have my own room to put all my things in?" Raghnall asked, replacing his glasses. "Do you have a lot of books?"

"You could stay in the garden shed until I figure out how to tell my parents about you," Ludlow said. "My nana uses it. I mean, she used to use it. She did a lot of gardening before she got... Well, nobody uses it anymore."

"Are there books in your garden shed?" he asked.

"I could bring you some," Ludlow answered.

"Cool," Raghnall said. "I'll just go tell her I'm not stopping here."

"Cool?" Ludlow repeated as Raghnall walked away

towards the fishing boat. "Did he just say 'cool'"? Ludlow asked, but Duchess only licked his face in response.

The scene that surrounded him seemed so surreal now. Goblins frolicked in the water, walked past him dragging huge remnants of the *Anathema* over the sand and into the trees, waxed the hull of the *Lyonesse* and sat on flat rocks enjoying jam and scone picnics. Just as he had days earlier, he found himself wondering if this was all really happening.

"Hello," an unfamiliar voice called to them from a distance, and suddenly none of it was happening anymore. "Hello," she called again.

Ludlow looked down the beach to see a woman and man in uniform walking towards them. He jumped up, panicked, looking every which way for the goblins, but they had vanished. In their place were crabs and grounded seagulls. He, Storey and Duchess were suddenly alone on that stretch of beach.

"What the devil?" Storey asked, shaking a crab from his trouser leg.

"Are you alright?" the woman called as they drew closer.

"What are they? Coastguard rescue?" Storey asked, as Ludlow and Duchess hurried to his side. "Now that we don't need rescuing anymore, we're rescued. That's life for you, isn't it?"

"Do you speak English?" the woman and man were almost face to face with them now.

"Yes," Storey said. "UK citizens as well. I've got my I.D. on the boat. We've just had a bit of a wreck, but I think we've got it sorted."

"Yeah, nasty bit of weather we had there," the man said. "We had reports of a vessel in distress. We were expecting a flaming shipwreck from the sounds of it, a tall ship they said, and turns out it was just your little fishing boat." The man took out a pen and a notepad and scribbled something in it as the woman asked them their names.

Neither one of them answered her. They were a bit distracted, you see. They had only now noticed that the debris from the *Anathema* had vanished just as the goblins had. Where there had once been planks of wood, barrels and swaths of the sails floating in the water, there were only clumps of seaweed, swirls of sea foam and a ridiculously out of place yellow and orange rubber duck.

"What's going on?" Storey asked, almost to himself.

"Are you sure you're alright?" the woman asked.

"Pardon?" Storey asked. "Oh, yes, yes, we're fine, thank you. Erm, how are you?"

The man scribbled wildly in his notebook.

"I asked for your names," the woman said.

"Oh, right, of course. Our names. I'm Michael Storey, of Mullion, and this..." Storey said, putting a hand on Ludlow's shoulder, "this is..."

"I'm his grandson," Ludlow answered.

Reader, while it is often best to tell the truth, when you have been kidnapped and held captive by creatures human beings don't believe in and escaped with the help of other creatures human beings don't believe in, it is preferable not to tell human beings the truth unless you are fairly certain that they will believe your story and not send you for years of psychological therapy. Even at eleven years old, Ludlow knew this. At Storey's age, he definitely would have known it.

"Yes," Storey said. "This is my grandson, Peter."

The man pulled a radio from his belt and spoke into it. "Yeah, it's just a fishing boat. Can you run the name Michael Storey, fisherman out of Mullion, and check that he has a grandson called Peter?"

"Last name also Storey?" the woman asked, and then, "Who's that?" she asked, looking up at the deck of the *Lyonesse*.

Ludlow and Storey looked up to see a young, blond-haired teenaged boy peering over the railing of the fishing boat before he dropped out of sight.

"Boy," the woman called.

He reappeared, hesitantly, trembling. Though it looked nothing like him, it could only have been Raghnall.

"My God," the man said.

"Isn't that...?" the woman started.

"We've got a situation here," the man said into his radio.

"Is that...?" Storey began.

"We rescued him," Ludlow said, almost shouting over Storey. "He was at sea, in a lifeboat."

"Is that true, son?" the woman called up to Raghnall.

"Yes," he said, nodding. "They rescued me."

"Forget the check on Michael Storey," the man said into his radio. "I'm gonna need you to run another name and bring the boat round the west side of the island..."

"What's going on?" Storey asked.

"We've been looking for him," the woman answered.

"I don't..." Storey started, removing his hat and scratching his head. "How can I put this? I don't think he is who you think he is."

The coastguard boat appeared from behind the edge of the treeline at the opposite end of the beach as the two officers climbed onto the deck of the *Lyonesse*.

Ludlow and Storey watched nervously, but their nervousness only turned to confusion at the sight of the smiles on the officers' faces, and then the most shocking thing that could have happened, did happen. They both hugged Raghnall.

"What's going on?" Ludlow asked.

"I don't know," Storey said. "Just when I think things can't get any more bizarre, they do."

The officers seemed to be asking Raghnall questions. Though Ludlow and Storey couldn't hear what they were saying, Raghnall seemed terribly confused and kept pressing his index finger to his forehead as he did when he was thinking hard about something.

The man finally jumped down onto the beach, speaking into his radio again. "He's a bit disoriented, but it's definitely him." He waved happily at two other officers on the deck of the coastguard boat, who waved back and then high-fived each other.

"Who do they think he is? The crown-flaming-prince or something?" Storey asked.

The man walked back towards them. "We'll be bringing him back with us," he said, reaching for Storey's hand and shaking it crazily. "Thank you for rescuing him. Will you be alright to get back on your own?"

"Erm, yes, I suppose," Storey answered.

"You're bringing him back?" Ludlow asked. "Back where?"

"Home, of course," the man answered, as if it was obvious.

The seagulls squawked and the crabs herded around them, seemingly in protest.

"Don't worry," he said, shooing the seagulls away with his hat. "We'll take good care of him."

Raghnall and the woman appeared behind him on the beach, with the woman carrying the library books under her arm. Raghnall still looked quite confused and his eyes were full of tears as he approached them.

"Thank you for everything," he said, as he reached out to shake Storey's hand. Storey took his hand and pulled him into a hug.

"You don't have to go with them," Storey whispered.

"Yes, I do," Raghnall answered. He turned to Ludlow next. With tears streaming down over his human cheeks, he reached for Ludlow's hand, and Ludlow hugged him too.

"You can't go," Ludlow said with a sniffle. "You're my best mate."

"You're my best mate, Lud," Raghnall answered into Ludlow's shoulder.

"Come now," the woman said, pulling tissues from her satchel and handing them around. "There's no need for tears. You'll see each other again, I'm sure."

Raghnall dropped to his knees and wrapped his arms around Duchess's neck, while she licked the side of his face and hair.

"Goodbye," he said.

A motorized inflatable dinghy landed on the beach behind them as the man asked Storey, "Are you sure you don't need a lift?"

"No," Storey answered. "Thank you. Boat's sorted,

course is set. I'll get him home."

Raghnall gave a last nod to Ludlow and Storey, lightly patted Ludlow's chest pocket, and finally turned away. As he followed the officers to the dinghy, the crabs and seagulls turned back into goblins, and the rubber duck disappeared beneath the surface of the water with a gentle splash. Ludlow peered into his pocket at Harry, who was still shivering slightly and wiping away tears herself.

"Harry, the enchantment's wearing off," Ludlow whispered, and when he looked up again, he was surrounded by seagulls and crabs once more.

"That's funny," Storey said, as Raghnall turned back to wave at them.

"What? It's not funny at all," Ludlow said.

"No, not actually funny. Strange, more like," Storey said.

"What is?"

"Well the fairy's spell, or whatever it is she does, wore off just then, but Raghnall didn't turn back into a goblin."

"You're right. That is strange," Ludlow agreed.

"What's funny is that she turned the mermaid into a rubber duck," he said. "I wish I could tell someone about it, but then I'd have to tell them everything else, and they'd think I'd finally lost my mind." He laughed and shook his head. "I'll miss that fairy's sense of humour. Won't you?"

CHAPTER 43

The sea was calmer than it had been since Ludlow's journey began, or maybe it only seemed that way. The *Lyonesse*, almost as good as new, had been gliding through the water alongside a pod of dolphins for nearly twenty minutes. They peeked their snouts out of the sea and seemed to smile at him before jumping sideways into the white water of the boat's wake. They didn't tire of jumping, and Ludlow didn't tire of watching them. They were ordinary, everyday dolphins, not extraordinary, except in the ordinary, everyday way all living creatures are.

Duchess put her paws up on the ledge next to him and looked over as well. She let out a playful bark and the dolphins suddenly scattered away, revealing a glimmer of turquoise scales just beneath the surface.

Isla? Ludlow wondered, and then, "Isla!" he shouted, leaning over the side of the fishing boat. "Isla!" he shouted a second time, and this time she seemed to hear him. Her head turned slightly towards the boat, and eventually she surfaced.

"Hello, Ludlow Osgoode," she said, looking straight ahead once more.

"Hello," he said. "Have you come to say goodbye?"

"No," she answered. "I just happened to be going this way."

"Oh," he said.

"I was going to ask if *you* were following *me*," she said.

"Following you?" he asked. "Why?"

"Perhaps to say, 'Thank you for saving my life, Isla,' or 'You were right, Isla. I did need help after all,'" she said.

"Oh," Ludlow said, and didn't say anything else for

a few moments. "Thank you for saving my life, Isla," he eventually said, and then, "You were right. I did need help after all."

Although her hair and face were dripping with seawater, and although she still wouldn't look directly at him, he could tell that she was crying. "We all need help sometimes," she said with a sniffle.

Ludlow only nodded.

"Well, I should be getting back now."

"I thought you were going this way," he said.

"Say goodbye to Michael Storey and Harry for me," she said, slowing and allowing the boat to overtake her.

"Wait," he said, running to the stern of the boat and leaning over the railing. "Will I ever see you again?"

"Maybe," she answered, finally looking him in the eyes, "but if not, it was grand to have known you, Ludlow Osgoode."

"It was grand to have known you!" he shouted back, as she disappeared into the water, her tail flicking against the surface at him for the last time before turning into a yellow and orange rubber duck and being pulled under.

"Harry," Ludlow said with a sigh. "Enough with the

rubber duck." He sniffled, then laughed. "Grand?" he said to himself. "I don't say 'grand.'"

It is worth noting that from that day forward, although he still didn't use it often, *grand* was Ludlow Osgoode's favourite word.

Duchess let out a whine and nudged Ludlow's arm as dogs do when they want a good scratch behind the ears, and Ludlow obliged her instead of wiping away his own tears.

"Weather's quite grey up ahead," Storey said, leaning out the wheelhouse door. "What on earth was that?" he asked. He jumped back into the wheelhouse and fidgeted with some levers, and the boat slowed to trolling speed. "Did you see it?" Storey asked, as he stepped back out onto the deck, looking every which way.

"See what?" Ludlow asked, finally wiping his face with the sleeve of his cardigan.

"It was some kind of bird," he said. "It was beautiful, glittering and shimmering. It moved so quickly, I thought it must be a hummingbird, but then it just disappeared into thin air."

"I didn't see it," Ludlow said, looking around himself.

"Are there hummingbirds in Europe?" he asked. "I don't think there are. Well, it couldn't have been a bird of any kind, could it? We're still too far from land. I swear," Storey said, "this whole adventure has made me see things that aren't there."

"It was probably a weejy weejy bird," Ludlow said.

"A whaty what?" Storey asked.

"A weejy weejy bird," Ludlow answered. "It really has vanished into thin air."

"A weejy weejy bird?" Storey asked, pulling off his hat and scratching his head, as he was becoming more and more accustomed to doing. "What the devil's a weejy weejy bird?"

"Look." Ludlow pointed towards the bow of the boat as another one approached and vanished before their eyes.

"Where's it gone?" Storey asked.

"Nobody knows where they go," Ludlow answered. "One minute they're here and then, *poof*, they're gone. You were lucky to have seen them before they disappeared."

CHAPTER 44

Dark cars lined the street in front of Ludlow's house. The day was as grey as the day he had left. He stood in the dripping rain, watching Storey's car disappear into the fog at the end of his road before pushing open the gate to his garden path.

As he approached the front door, he noticed that the spare room window was still open, in spite of the weather, and for some reason that even he didn't know, he decided to climb through it instead of ringing the doorbell. He landed face-first on the bed laden with his grandmother's coats and nestled into them as he had before. He lifted his head to see the room just as he had left it—the floor around her bed cluttered with half-packed boxes of her books and clothes, her dresser still overflowing with grainy old photographs of his grandfather, creams, perfumes and pill bottles.

As he looked up at her broken cuckoo clock on the wall, a little tear trickled down his warm cheek, but he swiftly wiped it away, rolled off of the mound of coats and made his way to the door.

As he turned the knob from inside, someone was turning it from outside.

"Ludlow," he heard his father's voice and then his round, smiling face appeared from behind the door.

"I'm here, Dad," Ludlow answered.

"I'm sorry, Lud," he said. "I said I'd be right back and forgot all about you."

"What?" Ludlow asked.

"There's just been so much going on," he said.

"But wasn't that days ago?" Ludlow asked.

"It does feel like it's been days, doesn't it?" his father answered. "Strange."

"Did you find him?" he heard his mother call.

"Yeah!" his father shouted, looking Ludlow up and down. "My God," he said, "What's happened to your shoes? There'll be no saving them."

Ludlow looked down at his wet mud-caked dress shoes.

"Faye!" his father shouted down the hall. "He's still damp with rain. Shall I find him some dry clothes?"

"No, you'll just choose something ugly," his mother answered from the kitchen, while some ladies quietly laughed. "I'll get to it in a minute."

"Yeah, she's probably right," his father said. "Just kick those shoes off and let's get you near the fire for now."

Ludlow emerged from the spare room to find his house still filled with the same people he had seen at his grandmother's funeral, the same people who had been there when he left, drinking tea and coffee and munching on devilled eggs and crustless sandwiches and talking in hushed voices among themselves.

"Why are all these people still here?" Ludlow asked, as he followed his father into the lounge.

"They'll be heading home soon enough," his father answered, switching on the television. "It's been a long day." The fire made a loud *pop*. "A very long day." He shook his head. "Take a seat here with Toby and watch some television. Your mother's just making a fresh pot of tea. We'll get you a cup in a minute."

Ludlow climbed onto his father's armchair and nestled in between the arm and the sleeping spaniel. The fire crackled and flared. Sparks jumped from the fireplace and fizzled out on the hearth.

"I still miss her, Dad," Ludlow whispered.

"You'll always miss her," his father answered. "We all will, but just think—you only miss her because you loved her so much, and that's a wonderful thing." He sat on the arm of the chair and gave Ludlow a pat on the head. "I'm sorry you've not had much of a birthday, Lud," he said.

"*Today's* my birthday?" he asked.

"Of course it is," he said. He looked at him with a curious expression. "Are you alright?"

"No," Ludlow answered, "but I will be."

"Of course you will. Don't forget, we've got each other. We'll all get through it together. You're not alone, after all."

His uncle burst into the room. "Do you believe this?" he asked, as he turned up the volume on the television. "Over two years he's been missing and the Coastguard's just discovered him on an island in the Celtic Sea."

"Who?" his father asked, as footage was shown of two familiar-looking Coastguard Rescue Service officers leaving a hospital car park.

"That boy. The one who went missing from the beach in Cornwall," his uncle said over the voice of the woman reading the news.

The boy, Ronald Maddock, previously of Morrab Road, Penzance, disappeared from Longrock Beach two years ago this month, when he went to scatter the ashes of his beloved dog, Belle.

A photograph of the boy appeared in the top right corner of the television screen.

Ludlow's mouth dropped open in disbelief. He pulled open his shirt pocket and peered down at the glowing ball of fairy that stared up at him, an apologetic look on her face and a shrug in her shoulders.

The child, now thirteen years old, has been taken to West Cornwall Hospital, where he is being treated for an undisclosed medical condition and interviewed by local authorities. Although little information is being released at this time, his attending doctors have indicated that the boy is expected to make a full recovery. His parents, Mark and Rosalyn Maddock, are at his bedside and have commented only that they are relieved to have him home.

One final thing you should know about goblins is that not all goblins started out that way.

"Raghnall?" Ludlow asked.

RONALD FOUND

If you're reading this, it's probably because you're interested in finding out what happens to Ludlow next, and you'll find out in spring 2019, with the release of book two of the Osgoode Odyssey:

FOOL'S FIRE

You also might be reading this because you don't have another book to move on to at the moment and are desperate for something else to read. Although this is a fairly serious dilemma, it can easily be remedied by a trip to your local bookstore or library.

Acknowledgments

Thanks to my husband, parents, family, friends and pets, past and present, for daily joy, laughter and happy memories.

Thanks to the teachers throughout my schooling who shared their passion for language and literature, especially Ms. Gordon, Ms. Saba, Mr. Leadbetter, Ms. Vineberg, Mr. Floen, Ms. Blond and Mr. McAuley.

Thanks to the authors for creating that literature in the first place.

Thanks to Noah Adam Paperman and Julie Prescesky for their talents and contributions.

Last, but by no means least, thanks to Alexa Nazzaro, without whose encouragement this book might never have been written, let alone published.

- Kate

MY GRANDMOTHER
AN ENTRY FROM MY DIARY

ON SUNDAY I WENT TO THE AIRPORT. IT TOOK ONE HOUR TO GET THERE.
WHEN WE GOT THERE, IT WAS ALMOST DARK. IT WAS VERY LATE. WE
WENT DOWN THE PATH AND UP STAIRS. WE WENT BECAUSE MY GRANDMOTHER
WAS COMING BACK FROM ENGLAND. EVERY SATURDAY I USED TO GO TO MY
GRANDMOTHER'S HOUSE. I COULDN'T GO TO SEE HER LATELY BECAUSE SHE
WAS IN ENGLAND. I ONLY HAVE SEVENTEEN DOLLARS AND HOW WOULD I
GET THERE? MY GRANDMOTHER IS VERY KIND. SHE LIKES TO PLAY GAMES
WITH MY SISTER AND ME. SHE TAKES US CAMPING AND SHOPPING, BUYS
US LOTS OF CLOTHES, STICKERS AND CANDY.

SHE LOVES US AND WE LOVE HER. AT THE AIRPORT, WE PLAYED GAMES,
THEN WE ATE. AS WE ATE WE SAW THAT AN AIRPLANE WAS COMING INTO
THE AIRPORT, AND IT WAS MY GRANDMOTHER'S PLANE. WE WENT TO THE
BIG, BIG, WINDOW TO WATCH FOR HER. SHE GOT OUT OF THE PLANE,
TOOK HER BAGS, AND WE ALL WENT HOME. AFTER THAT SHE SHOWED US
ALL THE THINGS THAT OUR UNCLES AND AUNTS AND COUSINS HAD BOUGHT
FOR US. I GOT SIX PACKS OF STICKERS AND A DRESS, A LOT OF CLOTHES,
A COLOURING BOOK AND A JUMBO PACK OF PENS. I GOT A DOLL TOO. YOU
KNOW, I THINK MY GRANDMOTHER IS THE NICEST GRANDMOTHER I HAVE EVER
HAD.

*Special thanks to Gerry and Bev Dunne for holding on to their
copy of this journal entry for all these years.*

About the Author

Kate Robinson Dunne's first published story was a journal entry about her grandmother that she wrote at the age of seven, and which was featured in her school board's literary anthology. Many stories read and written later comes *Ludlow Lost*, Dunne's first novel, still honouring her grandmother and the  grandchild who loved her so dearly. A sequel is slated for spring 2019.

She lives just north of her hometown of Montreal with her husband, two dogs and the fairy she keeps in her pocket.

CPSIA information can be obtained
at www.ICGtesting.com
Printed in the USA
LVOW10s0242231217
560622LV00012B/1104/P